A NIGHT WITHOUT STARS

JAMES HOWE is the award-winning author of numerous books for children, including the popular series about a dog, a cat, and a most unusual rabbit: *Bunnicula, Howliday Inn, The Celery Stalks at Midnight, Nighty-Nightmare* and *Return to Howliday Inn*, all available in Avon Camelot editions. He is also the author of the *Sebastian Barth* mystery series and *Morgan's Zoo.*

While researching his nonfiction work, *The Hospital Book*, a 1982 American Book Award nominee, the author interviewed a young burn patient who, Mr. Howe writes, "spoke of his difficult situation with the distilled clarity of a poet. The real 'Donald' became the inspiration for the fictional character in *A Night Without Stars* and it is because of him that this book came to be written at all."

James Howe lives with his wife and daughter in Hastings-on-Hudson, New York.

A NIGHT WITHOUT STARS

JAMES HOWE

AN AVON CAMELOT BOOK

AVON BOOKS
A division of
The Hearst Corporation
1350 Avenue of the Americas
New York, New York 10019

First Avon Camelot Printing: September 1993
First Avon Flare Printing: April 1985

CAMELOT TRADEMARK REG. U.S. PAT. OFF. AND IN OTHER COUNTRIES, MARCA REGISTRADA, HECHO EN U.S.A.

Printed in the U.S.A.

OPM 10 9 8 7 6 5 4 3 2

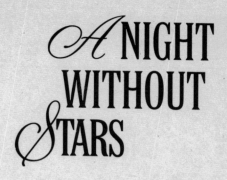

A NIGHT WITHOUT STARS

For Betsy, with my love,

and

For H.R., who is the reason

this book came to be

ACKNOWLEDGEMENTS

I am grateful to Nancy Lewis, Mary Jacobs, the Volunteer Department and the children of Bellevue Hospital; Tina Quirk and Betty Mann of Downstate Medical Center; Dr. Charles Fox and Eileen Savoy of the Burn Unit of Westchester Medical Center; Kathy McQuade, Dr. Lena Liu, Dr. Tom Elmquist, Joan Schmidt and Rita Conyers of St. Vincent's Hospital; John and Tessa Capodice, Jon Mazza, Joe and Tina Savarese, Rosa Vega and Betsy Imershein Howe for their generous help.

A NIGHT
WITHOUT
STARS

CARLO walked upside-down toward the two girls hanging on the jungle gym. They recognized him the instant they spotted his faded, hip-hugging jeans and the boldly emblazoned T-shirt which declared to the world: ¡Kiss me, I'm Italian!

"Maria!" Tina called, as she and Joni swung themselves upright. "Here comes your brother."

"He is *so* cute!" Joni gushed. "You know, I think I'm gonna marry him."

"Uh-uh," Tina objected, *"I'm* gonna marry Carlo. He's too good for you."

"Maria, who should marry Carlo? Me or Tina? Maria! Hey, Maria!"

Maria's long black hair, pulled back by crayon-shaped barrettes, framed her pale and worried face. From where she sat on a bench a few feet from her friends, she squinted in the summer sun and watched her brother approach. Carlo, here in the park in the middle of the day, could mean only one thing, she thought: trouble. She felt her heart racing inside her chest.

"Oh!" Tina cried out then. "He's coming closer! Look out below! I'm gonna faint, I can feel it. Oh, oh, oh, I'm dying!" Maria looked up as Tina dropped onto the sand at the bottom of the jungle gym and sprawled herself out, a victim to the arrows of unrequited crush.

"That's a good way to break your neck," Carlo remarked evenly as he joined the girls. Joni ignored the fact that he sounded exactly like an older brother and stretched her arms eagerly in his direction; her chubby hands flapped in the air like fat butterflies.

"Catch me, Car-r-r-lo," she cried out, rolling her *r*'s dramatically to sound Italian and glamorous, neither of which she was. "I'm falling! Help me! Help me! You don't want me to br-r-reak my neck, do you?"

"Hey, Joni," Carlo replied, "it sounds like you already broke your tongue, you know? What can I tell you?"

"Tell her that you love her," Tina shouted from the ground. No sooner had she said it than she began giggling wildly. Joni, stunned at first by Tina's brazenness, quickly gave in to a fit of laughing so boisterous the jungle gym started to rock.

Carlo looked at her and shook his head in disbelief. He turned to Maria. "Your friends are crazy," he said. "You know that, don't you?"

Maria smiled weakly and said nothing.

Suddenly, Joni felt herself slipping. *Really* slipping. "Oh, I'm falling!" she cried.

Carlo, thinking she was still playing, continued to shake his head and watch her.

"Ah . . . ah . . ." Joni whimpered, a frightened look coming over her as her hand let go of the pipe she'd been holding onto. Seeing that she really was in danger of falling, Carlo ran toward her and caught her in his arms. She looked up into his eyes and felt herself go red all over. She wasn't laughing anymore. And in about six seconds, she'd start hiccoughing.

Maria thought, they really *are* crazy! Don't they know how stupid they look, making such a fuss over Carlo? What's the big deal about boys anyway? It seemed like all of a sudden that was all Joni and Tina talked about. Her eyes drifted down to her feet, which were crossed at the ankles, and she stared at her new pink shoelaces, wondering when Carlo would tell her why he'd come. She knew, of course, but until he told her she could pretend it wasn't true.

Carlo set Joni on her feet; she pulled away as fast as she could and brushed herself off, even though she hadn't gotten the least bit dirty.

"Now you gotta marry him, Joni," Tina taunted, crawling through the bars of the jungle gym. "You *touched* each other."

"Shut up," Joni warned in a low voice. Her red was deepening to crimson.

"He held you in his arms!" Tina made a fluttering

motion over her heart and batted her eyelashes maniacally. Joni slugged her.

"I told you to shut up!" she roared.

"Ow!" Tina shrieked. "Now you've asked for it."

Tina was bigger than Joni and it was a known fact that when she was angry she hit harder than anybody —boy or girl—in the sixth grade. And now she was angry.

"Oh, oh," Joni said between hiccoughs. "See ya, Maria." And she was off, Tina fast on her heels.

"Later!" Tina called out to Maria as she tore after Joni. They ran off in the direction of the big tree at the end of the pond and disappeared behind the rec hall.

After watching them go, Carlo leaned against the jungle gym; he looked down at the top of Maria's head. She mumbled something. "What?" Carlo asked.

Maria looked up and squinted into the sun. "I said, 'They're so dumb,'" she replied, but that really wasn't what she'd said at all. She'd really asked, "What are you doing here?"

A FEW minutes later, Maria and Carlo stood by Fisheye Freddy's cart eating hot dogs with lots of mustard and sauerkraut. Maria drank a Dr. Pepper; Carlo preferred canned iced tea. "All that soda junk is no good for you," he always said, ignoring the list of chemicals on the side of the iced tea can in his hand.

All the kids called Freddy "Fisheye" because he had

these big eyes that popped out at you and his mouth looked like it was always saying "oh" even when it wasn't. Maria's friend, Marlene, who was twelve-going-on-thirteen and wore a bra and was therefore considered to be a world-authority on all sorts of things, said that his mouth got that way from eating so many hot dogs. But Maria didn't believe that. She figured it was genetic, although she wasn't sure what that meant.

Right now, she wasn't thinking about Fisheye Freddy, though. She was wondering when Carlo would drop the bomb.

"Good hot dog?"

Maria nodded.

"Want another?"

She nodded again, and Carlo ordered two more, with everything. Fisheye Freddy smiled roundly and said, "Gee, the little one really likes them franks, don't she?" Maria rolled her eyes upward and moved away to a nearby bench. After a moment, Carlo joined her. He extended her second hot dog and sat down.

"I was home just now," he said.

Here it comes, Maria thought. She felt her stomach tighten and wished she hadn't asked for the second hot dog. Her heart started beating fast again, too. Stop it, heart! she commanded. But that heart of hers did whatever it wanted.

"And while I was there—" Carlo went on.

"Where was Mommy?" Maria asked, interrupting. "Wasn't she home?"

"Sure, she was there. Let me tell you, will you?"

"Okay."

"I went home for lunch, like I always do. Only I didn't get to eat because the phone rang, and when I answered it—"

"Why didn't Mommy answer it?" Maria asked.

"She was busy with Anna, giving her a bath or something." Anna was their baby sister. Ever since the hot weather had set in this summer, she had been suffering from a heat rash that had transformed her from a pleasant-tempered little kid into a nonstop screaming machine. She was driving everyone crazy. And between that and toilet training, she was keeping their mother busy all day long.

"Anyway, I picked up the phone and it was the hospital."

Maria put her uneaten hot dog down on the bench. She sat very still and listened.

"See, the thing is . . ." Carlo said, looking straight at Maria, who was looking straight at her pink shoe-laces again, "they want you to come in tomorrow. They've got a bed for you, see, and they're planning to do the operation in a couple days."

Maria's throat tightened so that it was hard to swallow. It was funny how she became so aware of that just then. That and her eyes. They seemed stuck open, like they couldn't, or wouldn't, blink. It was as if all the normal things her body should have been doing by itself shut down. She was caught, suspended somewhere between a blink and a swallow.

Carlo was saying something about how he was going to take part of the day off from work ("You don't have to do that," she heard herself object, even though she was really glad he would be there) and how their mother would leave Anna with Mrs. O'Hearn next door so that together they could take her to DeWitte Hospital in the morning.

DeWitte was the hospital in Manhattan to which Maria had gone a month before for the big examination (a cardiac catheterization, it was called). Even though her family had lived in Queens for three years now, she still went to the heart clinic at DeWitte every six months. So it made sense that's where she'd go for the operation.

"What do you think?" Carlo asked. Maria noticed that he'd stopped eating his hot dog, too. He held it in his open hand, which rested on his knee.

Maria shrugged. "Nothin'," she replied after a moment.

"You okay?"

"Sure, I'm okay. Why shouldn't I be?" She wasn't going to let Carlo see how scared she was. She really looked up to her oldest brother, and she knew he was crazy about her. She wanted him to be proud of her, not think she was a baby like Anna, crying all the time.

[9]

"You're sure you're all right?" Carlo asked then.

"I said so, didn't I?" Maria mumbled.

"Okay, okay." Carlo took a bite of his hot dog. Maria just looked at hers, lying on the bench, and left it there. The way she was feeling, her stomach all tied up in knots, she was afraid if she ate it, she might throw up or something.

"Aren't you going to be late getting back to work?" she asked her brother suddenly.

"I got a couple minutes yet. Anyway, the boss is a good guy. He'd understand."

Maria was glad to be talking about something else. "You like this job, Carlo?"

It was Carlo's turn to shrug. "It's a job," he said. "Seems kind of crazy to go to school till I'm eighteen just so I can work in a dry-cleaning plant when I'm nineteen." He looked off into the distance, then back at Maria, breaking into the smile that made him look like a movie star and explained why all of Maria's friends had crushes on him. "Hey, listen, go figure. It's a mixed-up world, right?" He tousled Maria's hair, and she felt her body relax.

"Tell you what we're gonna do, you and me."

"What?" Maria asked, leaning her head on Carlo's arm.

"We're going to get us a car, that's what."

Maria pulled away and looked up at her brother. "Talk about something we'll really do, not make-believe," she said.

"I'm talkin' really."

"You're supposed to be saving money for college. How're you going to buy a car? Anyway, what's wrong with Daddy's car?"

"Dad's car is his car. I want us to have our own. Besides, it won't cost me that much. I'll get a junker and fix it up myself. Put in a CB and an eight-track, and then I'll put the name on the side for the whole world to see."

"What name?"

" 'Easy Goin'.' "

" 'Easy Goin'?' " Maria laughed.

"Yeah, what's wrong with that? It's a good name."

"It's a funny name."

"Well, sorry to hear you think so. I like it."

"Oh, Carlo, I'm just teasing. It's a nice name. Really." Maria smiled and leaned back against Carlo's arm again. She closed her eyes and felt the sun warm her face.

"We'll be able to go anywhere we want, whenever we want," Carlo went on. "Free as the breeze. 'Easy Goin'.' Get it?"

"Uh-huh," Maria murmured.

Carlo glanced at his watch. "Well, I better get back to work, I guess. I'll see you home later, okay?"

Maria felt the kiss on the top of her head and the shift of her brother's body as he rose from the bench.

"Oh, oh," he said, looking off to his left. Two bubble-gum-chewing roller skaters were wheeling rapidly in his direction. "Here come your nutso friends again. I don't think I can take them more than once a day." He looked back at Maria and noticed the worried look in her eyes.

The sound of roller skates on concrete grew louder. "Gotta make my getaway," he said. "I'll see you later."

"Yeah."

"*Ciao,*[1] kiddo."

"Bye, Carlo."

"Maria! Maria!" Joni and Tina called out. "Get your skates. We'll wait for you." They pulled up in front of her. Joni blew a huge pink bubble that exploded all over her nose and chin. Maria and Tina laughed.

"So come on, Maria, go get your skates."

Maria knew she couldn't, that, like so many things these days, roller skating tired her out and made her heart feel weird.

"No," she said, "I don't feel like it right now. You guys go ahead, though. I'll watch."

Joni, picking the gum off her face, gave Maria a funny look. What was with her these days, anyway? She never liked to do anything. With a shrug, she said, "C'mon, Tina, let's go."

Maria watched as they skated away and became very small in the distance.

"A HOLE in your heart?" Joni uttered in disbelief. "Oh, Maria, why didn't you tell us before?"

[1] So long.

"Yeah, Maria," Tina joined in. "We're supposed to be your best friends, after all."

Roller skates slung over their shoulders, the girls walked slowly up Parsons Boulevard, heading back to Tina's house to watch "A Better Life," their favorite soap opera.

"You knew there was something wrong with my heart," Maria replied softly. "I told you that a long time ago. You know I go to the clinic, right?"

"Yeah."

"And you know I was in the hospital last month, don't you?"

"Right, but that was just for a couple of days. Anyway . . ."

"Anyway, you never told us it was a hole in your heart."

"Yeah." It was Tina speaking again. "That's terrible. You could die from that, right?"

"Shut up, Tina," Joni hissed. "You want to scare her?"

"But you could, right? I mean, if you've got a hole in your heart, all your blood could leak out."

"You don't see any blood leaking out of me, do you?" Maria snapped.

"No, but it wouldn't work that way. It would leak into your body and pretty soon you'd be all filled up with blood like a sponge."

"Tina!" Joni squealed. She stopped herself from

punching her friend in the arm, since her own arm was still sore from their earlier exchange.

The girls turned the corner onto Oak Avenue. Tina's house was the last one on the block. They were walking slowly now; there was plenty of time before "A Better Life" began.

"What are they going to do to you anyway?" asked Joni.

"I don't know exactly," Maria replied. "They're going to open my heart up, I know that."

Unable to contain herself, Tina wrinkled her face up like a prune. "Ooooo," she said, "that's *so* gross." Joni shot her a look, then turned back to Maria.

"Yeah? And then what?"

Maria looked blankly into the faces of her two friends. Their eyes were wide with wonder. As they came to the front steps of Tina's house, they sat down.

"I don't know," said Maria after a moment.

"Didn't the doctor tell you anything?"

Maria tried to remember. "He said I was going to have open-heart surgery, that's all. He didn't tell me what it means."

"If *I* were going to have an operation," Tina said, "I wouldn't *want* to know any of the bloody details. Just knock me out and don't tell me a thing."

"Not me," Joni said. "After all, it's my body. I'd want to know. Hey, here comes Marlene. Let's ask her, okay, Maria?"

"Ask her what?"

"If she knows what they're going to do to you. Marlene knows all kinds of stuff."

Marlene walked slowly toward the group on the steps. She was wearing bright red shorts and a tight T-shirt that let you see clearly she was wearing a bra underneath. Marlene was okay, Maria thought, but she'd become something of a pain since she started wearing that bra.

"What's up?" Marlene's open-mouthed gum-chewing and half-lidded stare made her look like she was bored out of her mind. She sighed heavily.

"Maria has a hole in her heart," Tina blurted out.

"She's going to have open-heart surgery," Joni added.

"Oh, yeah?" Marlene snapped her gum and blinked once, slowly, as if she'd just been told nothing more fascinating than the time of day. "They'll probably have to give her a new heart," she said casually.

"What?" This was too much for Tina. "What do you mean, a new heart?"

"Didn't you ever hear of heart transplants?"

"Well, yeah."

"Sure, but—"

"They can't fix a hole in your heart," Marlene asserted knowingly. "They have to give you a new one."

"Where would they get a new heart?" Joni asked. All three girls stared at Marlene.

"Well, it won't be new really. More like used."

"Huh?"

"I don't understand," Joni said. But Maria was

beginning to, and she wasn't sure she wanted to hear any more.

"From a dead person, silly," Marlene whispered.

"Oh, *gross!*" was Tina's response.

"They'll take Maria's heart out, see, and put in a heart from somebody who just kicked the bucket."

"But whose heart would they use?"

"Anybody's. It doesn't matter."

"Oh, no." Tina was close to tears now. She turned to Maria, a look of horror sweeping across her face. "What if they give her the heart of a murderer? Or a drug addict?"

"Or somebody who isn't Catholic?" Joni added.

"Yeah, I hadn't thought of that!" said Tina.

"Listen, you dopes," Marlene, authority on transplant surgery, continued, "don't worry about that stuff. Just hope she gets through the operation. It's very dangerous, you know."

"You mean she might not live?" Tina asked. The way they were talking now, it was as if Maria were no longer there. She sat, listening to her fate being tossed around like an old tennis ball.

"I'm not saying that. It's just dangerous, that's all."

Tears began to roll down Tina's face. "I'll *die* if Maria isn't in my class next fall. I just will. Seventh grade is supposed to be the best, and I won't enjoy it at all if Maria isn't there."

"Me, either," Joni said. She wasn't crying, but her face was getting a little white.

"Look, I'm not saying she's going to die. It's just dangerous, that's all. Maria knows that, right, Maria? Your doctor told you all this, didn't he?"

"I guess," Maria answered, not at all sure any longer what her doctor had told her. She knew one thing: he'd never told her they were going to give her somebody else's heart.

"I *knew* I didn't want to hear any of this," Tina said. "It's so gross."

She and Joni gazed at Maria, and then Joni reached out and touched her arm. "You are so brave," she said.

"Yeah, like a saint," Tina added wistfully. "Saint Maria."

"Oh, my gosh," said Marlene suddenly. She was looking at her watch.

"What?"

" 'A Better Life' started already. Let's go."

Tina ran ahead of the others. "I hope they didn't tell yet if Krissi's husband was killed in the car crash."

"Me, either," Joni joined in. "I want to see the expression on her face when they tell her. Come on, Maria."

Maria watched her friends disappear into the house and walked slowly up to the front door.

Brave, she thought, as if I have a *choice.* Then, lifting her eyes to the sky above, she thought: it's not fair, God, I didn't ask to be a saint.

TWO

MARIA, call your brother down for supper. Your papa and Carlo will be home any minute. And, Maria . . ."

"What, Mommy?"

"Don't run up those stairs. You know it isn't good for you. Just call."

Mrs. Tirone went back into the kitchen as Maria pulled the corners of her mouth back, tight. Why did her mother have to treat her like a baby? Don't climb. Don't run. Don't jump. What fun was it living in a two-story house if you couldn't race up the stairs two at a time?

It hadn't always been that way. It was just in the past few months, ever since she'd started having more of a problem with her heart. What did they think, anyway? That she'd have a stroke and die? The thought startled Maria into a new one: what if she *did* have a stroke and die?

Of course, Maria thought then, maybe her mother was treating her like a baby because lately she'd been acting more like one. Since coming home from the hospital last month she'd been calling her mother "Mommy" instead of "Mom." And one night, she even wet the bed. Eleven years old and she wet the bed! She just about died of embarrassment from that one, but fortunately, her mother never said a word to anyone else. "It will be our little secret," she told Maria. God, if Joey had found out . . . She could just imagine what mileage he would have gotten out of it.

"Joey!" Maria called.

No answer. How could he hear her anyway with his radio blasting the way it was? She tried again.

"Jo-eee! Supper!"

Nothing. She sneaked a peek at the kitchen door. Her mother was nowhere in sight. Skipping every other step, she zoomed up to Joey's and Carlo's room and pounded on the door. The loud thumping of her fist sounded the way her heart felt inside her chest.

The door flew open. Joey glared at her from the other side. Hair slicked back with grease, his white shirt open to the third button to show off his Medal of the Blessed Mother, black pants tapering down to black shoes polished to a fine shine, he was a vision. His shoes weren't the only thing about him with a shine, Maria noticed; a brand new pimple glowed like a headlight on the tip of his nose.

"Oh, boy, aren't you pretty?" Maria said.

"What?"

She smirked and raised her voice. "Turn down the radio, and you'll be able to hear!"

"What have you got to say that I need to hear?" Joey shouted back.

Maria mouthed the words, "You've got a pimple on your nose."

"Huh?"

"I said, 'It's time for supper.' Get washed," Maria shrieked.

"Oh."

"Maria! Joey! Stop that yelling. It's not good for you, Maria. And turn that music off, Joey. Come to supper!"

Maria could hear Anna screaming in the kitchen. Sometimes, she thought, she was glad she wasn't her mother. Her life sure wasn't easy. Of course, sometimes she wished she weren't herself. Going into the hospital to have your heart opened up wasn't so easy either. Who would she like to be? she often asked herself. But she hadn't figured out an answer to that one. At least, not yet.

THE TIRONE family sat wordlessly around the table that night. Even Anna was still for a change. Forks and knives and ice-filled glasses tinkled and clinked like summer wind-chimes on a distant breeze. Maria ate the entire meal holding her breath. Or at least it felt that way. When was someone going to speak?

"Salt."

Maria looked across the table at her father and passed him the saltshaker. "Salt" was one of the four words (or five, depending on how you counted) her father used at the table. The others were "pepper," "butter" and " 'ts good."

The rules of the Tirone dinner table were simple and unstated. First, no one was to mention anything that might upset their father who, it was always assumed, had had a hard day at work. And second, there was to be no fighting or raising of voices. These rules seriously limited discussion and usually meant that either Carlo entertained everyone with stories from the plant or Joey and Maria, at their mother's urging and in as few words as possible, told everything that had happened to them in school that day. With school out for the summer and Carlo in an uncharacteristically quiet mood, Maria was sure they'd finish dessert and the only words she would hear the whole time would be "salt," "pepper," "butter" and " 'ts good."

But then Joey broke the silence.

"Since Maria's going into the hospital tomorrow," he said, "can I sleep in her room?"

Maria could feel her throat close around the lima beans that had been fighting their way down. "I *am* coming back, you know," she said after swallowing.

"I know that. I mean, while you're gone."

"Joey, eat your dinner!" Mrs. Tirone ordered, shaking her head. "Your sister's having a big operation. This isn't the time to ask about sleeping in her room."

"But if she isn't going to be here—"

"That's enough," Mrs. Tirone said sharply.

"Anyway, it's not fair she has her own room and I have to share," Joey muttered.

Carlo leaned back in his chair, reached around Maria and grabbed Joey by the shoulder.

"Huh?" Joey grunted, feeling his brother's firm grasp.

"Cool it, bro," was all Carlo said. Joey resumed eating, and the family fell silent again.

After a few minutes, Mrs. Tirone sighed and, raising her eyebrows mournfully, looked across the table at her oldest daughter. "Ai, Maria, Maria," she uttered. She shook her head and stared down at her plate. Maria looked from her mother to her father, who remained impassive.

"Don't worry, Mom," Carlo said then. "Dr. Whelan is a good doctor. He'll take care of our Maria."

"Oh, yes, I know that," agreed Mrs. Tirone. "I'm not worried."

Why not? Maria wanted to say. *I* am.

"It's just . . ." Maria's mother's voice trailed off. Looking up, she said, "You're right, Carlo. Dr. Whelan is a fine doctor." Then, suddenly putting on a smile, she added, "And so beautiful, eh?"

Joey laughed. "Beautiful?" he asked.

Blushing, Mrs. Tirone explained, "I mean like a TV doctor. His hair is nice and wavy, with just a little gray at the temples. And he's so tan."

"He can afford to be," Carlo interjected.

"He has a good, square jaw, too," Mrs. Tirone went on. "I like that a man has a good, square jaw."

Maria glanced at her father, who did not have a good, square jaw. She wondered what he thought of what her mother was saying. All at once, he looked up, glanced around and opened his mouth to speak.

"Butter," he said. Joey passed him the butter.

Mrs. Tirone continued. "He's not like that Dr. Collins at the clinic. I never liked him."

"You only met him once," Carlo reminded his mother. Since Anna was born, it had been Carlo who took Maria to the clinic, not their mother.

"His hands were wet. He was nervous, you know the type. I like that Dr. Whelan better. He's got a dry handshake. Yes. If we just believe in God and Dr. Whelan, our Maria will be fine." And now it seemed that whatever doubts may have been plaguing Mrs. Tirone had been put to rest.

Maria wasn't sure whom she liked better. Dr. Collins was friendlier, she knew that. He was young, and she enjoyed the way he kidded around with her. It was funny, though, that even with the joking, he seemed to take more of an interest in her, to really care what happened. After all, it was because of him she had gone to see Dr. Whelan in the first place and the decision had been made to have the operation. One thing she knew for certain: she would never decide that somebody was a better doctor because his hands were drier. Grown-ups sure were strange sometimes. Especially parents.

She had missed some of what was being said, but she did hear her mother say, "We'll all pray for Maria. We'll pray that everything will be all right."

"I'm going out," Joey said, pushing away from the table.

"Got a date?" Carlo asked. Joey reddened and said nothing.

"You can go out after you clean the dishes," was Mrs. Tirone's response.

Maria looked up. "That's my job," she said, annoyed. "Joey doesn't have to do it, I will."

"Now, Maria," her mother said patiently. "We've been through this before. It's not good for you . . ."

"You never let me do anything anymore," Maria said, raising her voice. "I'm not helpless, you know."

"Yeah," Joey agreed, "Maria never has to do anything around here. And I get stuck with girls' jobs like clearing the dishes."

"Now, Joey . . ."

"It's not fair," Joey continued. He pushed back his chair and stood, his anger rising with him. "Just 'cause Maria has a little problem with her heart—"

"Little problem?" Maria blurted out.

"Yeah," Joey said. "You think you're too good to work anymore?"

"No, I don't, smarty-pants. If Mommy would let me—"

"Maria! Joey! No fighting," Mrs. Tirone reprimanded. "Now, stop it! It's no good for Maria."

"You don't have to keep saying that, Mommy. I'm not an invalid, you know. Really, I'm okay." Maria felt her heart racing inside her chest. Just as she thought she might explode, a scream erupted from Anna.

"Now, look what you've done," Mrs. Tirone said to Joey as she picked up the crying child.

"Look what I've done?" Joey cried. "Sure, sure, everything's my fault. Everything is always my fault!" He bolted from the table and ran out the front door.

Maria noticed that her father was silently eating the last of the meat loaf on his plate, not looking at anyone. How does he stay so calm? she wondered.

Carlo tapped her on the shoulder.

"Want to help me?" he asked. "You take the glasses. I'll take the plates."

MARIA knocked softly on her parents' bedroom door.

"Come in," her mother's voice invited.

"I can't sleep," Maria said, standing in the darkness by her mother's side of the bed. She loved the smell of lilacs in this room. And the cool, silky softness of the sheets. She wished she could sleep in here tonight, just tonight. She wanted to lie in the valley between her mother and father, be safe there, smell the lilacs until sleep came.

Her mother stroked her hand gently for a long time. "You want me to sing to you?" she asked at last.

Maria nodded her head, but her mother couldn't see.

"Eh?"

"Yes."

"Come."

Her father stirred in his sleep as they left the room. Moments later in Maria's room, Mrs. Tirone rubbed her daughter's back as she sang to her.

> *Sleep, my love, and peace attend thee,*
> *All through the night.*
> *Guardian angels God will send thee*
> *All through the night.*

"Mommy?"

"Mmmm?"

"Nothing bad will happen to me, will it?"

"No, no, no. Nothing bad. God will watch over you."

"And you?"

"Yes, God will watch over me, too. He watches over everyone."

"No, I mean, will you watch over me, too?"

"Oh, yes. Yes, of course."

Rolling onto her back, Maria looked up at her mother. With the moonlight casting its shadows and a long, loose strand of hair gliding down the side of her face, she looked like a madonna in a painting. Maria smiled at the thought; always before her mother had looked like a mother, never a madonna.

"I hope when I grow up I'm pretty like you," she said.

"Why, thank you, Maria. But I think you're very pretty right now."

"Really?"

"Mm-hmm."

"The operation won't make me ugly, will it?"

"Tsk, Maria, why should it make you ugly?"

Maria imagined a hideous, bumpy scar running down her chest. She saw herself as a freak, laughed at by the other kids when they went swimming. She silently vowed she would never again wear a bathing suit.

"Will it hurt when they cut me open?"

Mrs. Tirone winced at the thought of the scalpel touching her daughter's skin. "You'll be sound asleep," she said. "You won't feel a thing."

"But what if I wake up?"

"You won't . . ."

"And what if they give me the heart of a bad person? Marlene said—"

"Marlene said? Is that what's putting such ideas into your head? What does Marlene know? You believe your friends when you should believe the doctor."

"But the doctor hasn't told me anything."

"He's told you what you need to know."

"But, Mommy—"

"And what you don't know won't hurt you. Just have faith, Maria. Like I do. Remember: when you don't know, when you can't know, that is the time for faith. God *will* take care of you. Now, close your eyes and go to sleep. That's what you need more than anything. Sleep."

Looking into her mother's eyes, Maria wished she wouldn't keep telling her to leave everything to God. What if while she was having her operation God was busy with someone else?

When she closed her eyes to try to sleep, she saw herself lying on the operating table. "Tell me again it won't hurt," she said.

"You be a big girl, and nothing will hurt you."

Maria was startled to hear her father's voice. She opened her eyes and made out his shadowy figure in the doorway.

"You be brave," he said, his voice gruff from sleep. "Nothing bad is gonna happen to our Maria 'cause she's a big girl, eh?"

"Yes, Maria," her mother said then. "Now, sleep. Sleep. Nothing bad is going to happen."

An hour later, Maria was still awake. Her parents had gone back to their own room. To the lilac smells and the cool, soft sheets. Maria sat cross-legged on her bed, staring at the suitcase she and her mother had packed earlier.

What if I die? she thought. What will that be like? I won't be here anymore. Anna won't have a big sister. And Carlo will take Joey for rides in his car instead of me. I know Carlo likes me better than Joey, but if I'm dead, what choice will he have?

She looked up and saw her reflection in the mirror on her dresser. Pretty, she thought, that's what Mommy said. But will I be pretty after? Her eyes drifted down to the bottom edge of the mirror. The wooden frame cut her off right at her shoulders. She was relieved. She didn't want to have to check for the beginnings of breasts as she did so often these days when studying her image in the mirror. Because if she looked tonight, all she'd be able to see would be the scar. Even though it was hard for her to imagine what it would really look like.

She thought about Joni and Tina then, about how lucky they were to have nothing more to worry about than when their breasts were going to start growing and when they'd have boyfriends. Maria had begun to wonder about those things, too, in recent months, but now she had bigger worries, worries her friends couldn't begin to understand. What was going to happen to her anyway?

Have faith, her mother had said. When you don't know, have faith. But having faith wasn't such an easy thing. It wasn't like when she was little and went to church and said her prayers. Because then everything went the way it was supposed to, and nothing went wrong. And even though she'd always known her heart wasn't normal, she'd just lived with it. She'd thought she always could. But now . . .

She closed her eyes and listened. The house was very still. Please God, she whispered inside her head, help me have faith and don't let me die. And please don't let me be a freak that the other kids will laugh at. And don't let it hurt too much, God. Be there for me, okay, God? Be there like Mommy says you will.

Maria crawled back under the covers. As she drifted to sleep, the moonlight slipped through a tear in her window shade. It fell across her body and severed the darkness like a knife.

THREE

E NTERING DeWitte Hospital was like trying to squeeze into last summer's bathing suit after you'd grown during the year. Whoever had designed the place seemed to have forgotten when he got to the narrow doorway that on one side was New York, a very big city full of people needing to get in, and on the other, DeWitte Hospital, a very big place full of people wanting to get out. Going in either direction you had to scrunch yourself up to avoid being crushed. At least you did if you were Maria's size.

"Paging Dr. Colby. Dr. Colby, pick up 4871, please. Dr. Colby, 4871."

Bells rang. Elevator lights flashed. Voices shook and quivered. The stifling summer air gave way in a burst to air-conditioned chaos.

"Code Six. A Code Six on Five North. Code Six on Five North."

Carlo, suitcase swinging from his hand, was on one side of her; her mother was on the other. They stopped to ask a guard where the Admitting Office was, turning in the direction of his arrowed hand.

Bells and more bells rang.

"Dr. Whelan. Paging Dr. Birch Whelan . . ."

"Hey, Maria," Carlo said, "that's your doctor."

"Yeah, I know," Maria mumbled. Big deal, she thought. What did Carlo think? That just because her doctor's name was being said over the loudspeaker, he was famous or something? Maria sighed. Why was she feeling so nasty toward Carlo? It wasn't his fault she was here. It was no one's fault, she told herself, no one's fault.

". . . pick up 4858. Dr. Whelan, 4858."

Maria looked down at her feet as they moved along the corridor. There were fewer people here than in the main waiting room. As the voices receded behind her, she could hear the squeaking of her rubber soles on the marble floor. She glanced to one side and noticed a water fountain. She was thirsty, but didn't stop to drink. Who knew what diseases you could catch drinking from a hospital water fountain? On the other side of the hall she saw a door with a wooden bottom and a glass top.

"Admitting" it said in big gold letters on the glass part. Carlo opened it, and they went in.

The lady behind the desk asked Maria's mother a lot of questions, mostly about how they were going to pay. Mrs. Tirone didn't always answer with words. Instead, she put a few cards in front of the lady, who copied some numbers from them and gave them back. That seemed to be answer enough. Then the lady, who was big and puffy and didn't seem to have a name, put a plastic bracelet on Maria's wrist and told her mother that they should wait "over there."

"Over there" was a part of the room with red plastic couches, green plastic plants and a round glass and chrome table covered with magazines for grown-ups. Maria looked for something to read, but the only thing for kids she could find was a Richie Rich comic book, and it was being read at the moment by an old man who whistled as he breathed. Maria wasn't sure why such an old guy would be reading Richie Rich, but she figured he was enjoying himself because every once in a while he'd let out a little wheezy chuckle. And then he'd sigh and whistle and very slowly turn a page.

So she decided she'd have to find something else to pass the time. Maybe she'd get Carlo to play Hangman with her. She liked that game. It was a special favorite during social studies class when she and Tina needed something, anything, to stave off death from boredom.

Before she had a chance to think much more about it, however, she felt a hand on her shoulder and heard a voice say, "Maria?"

Startled, she looked up to see a woman's eyes peering at her over the top of tiny black-rimmed glasses perched at the end of a tiny nose. The woman appeared to be about fifty. Her perfectly lipsticked lips parted to speak again.

"Are you Maria Tirone?"

"Yes."

"I thought so. I'm Miss Farrell. If you and your mother and . . ."

"Carlo," Carlo said. "I'm her brother."

"Yes," said Miss Farrell, straightening to her full height. She tugged at her pink smock, clutching a file-folder to her chest. "If you and your mother and brother will follow me, please, I'll take you to your room."

Walking back through the noisy main waiting room, Maria couldn't help wishing that someone other than Miss Farrell were taking her to her room. She was such a cold fish; she hadn't said two words the whole way to the elevator. Maria looked up at the file-folder Miss Farrell held so firmly against her body. She guarded it like it was top secret or something.

"What's in the folder?"

Miss Farrell looked down; she seemed surprised that someone had spoken to her.

"This is your health record," she answered tightly, after a moment's pause.

"Oh," Maria said. Then she added, "I used to call them 'vanilla folders.' "

"I beg your pardon."

"You know, *vanilla* folders. What my health record is in. They're really called 'manilla' folders, I know, but the first time I heard my teacher say it, I thought she said 'vanilla', so that's why I always called them 'vanilla folders.' "

Miss Farrell looked blankly at Maria. "Oh, I see," she said after a moment. "Ah-ha. Yes. I get it."

They stood before a row of elevators. Maria wished one would hurry up and come. When it did, she stepped in, only to be quickly squashed between Carlo and her mother. Her face was pressed against Miss Farrell's smock. She hated being crammed into the elevator like this. It reminded her of the last time she was in the hospital, riding on a stretcher-bed to the cardiac catheterization lab, staring up at the elevator ceiling, people pressing in around her. She'd felt frightened and hot and alone. The rubbery smell, as she'd gotten off the elevator, had sickened her. She'd forgotten all about that smell until now. Now, she remembered, too, the pain she'd felt after the test, the throwing up, the stiffness in her leg that had lasted for days.

And the nurses. Some of them had been okay. But there was one: "Gotta Lotta" she had nicknamed her, because she said "gotta lotta" all the time and because . . . well, because she really did have a lotta . . . fat, that is. Oh please, God, Maria thought, don't let Gotta Lotta be here this time. I don't like her, God. I know it's not nice, but I don't.

With a "ping," the elevator door opened. "This is us," Miss Farrell said. "Seventh floor. Peds."

"Huh?" Carlo asked.

"Peds. Pediatrics. The children's floor."

"Oh."

Maria looked around. She didn't immediately recognize any of the nurses.

Miss Farrell called down the hall. "Miz Fielding. Darlene, dear."

"Yes'm," came back a disembodied voice.

"New admission for you."

"All right. I'm comin', I'm comin'."

A large mass of weight rounded a corner and lumbered down the hall toward them.

"Well, well, well," Miz Fielding said, taking the folder from Miss Farrell. "Look who's here. Maria Angelina Tirone. You gotta lotta name there, chile. Ain't that the truth?"

Maria groaned.

"What's the matter, dear? Are you feeling ill?" Miss Farrell asked.

"Oh, no. No, I'm okay."

Maria smiled a kind of sickly smile as she looked up. It had to be. It was. Miz Fielding was just a code name for the one, the only, Gotta Lotta.

"MARIA Angelina Tirone. That's a pretty name."

"Thank you, sir."

The plump young doctor glanced up from where he sat at the end of Maria's bed, one leg tucked under him in an effort to appear casual. A clipboard teetered on a chubby thigh.

"You don't have to call me sir," he said. "My name is Dr. Landra. Or you can call me Bob."

"Yes, sir," Maria replied. She wasn't going to call him Bob, she knew that. He was a doctor, after all, even if he didn't look much like one. He had this shock of frizzy hair that made him look like he'd just stuck his finger in a wall socket. A cherub's features, round, pink and innocent, distinguished his face, making Maria think that without his wire-rimmed glasses and day-old growth of whiskers, he'd closely resemble Anna. Particularly now, with his brow furrowed the way it was and his cheeks all puffed out in intense concentration, he reminded her of Anna straddling her potty, determined to master the fine points of toilet training.

Everything he wore was white. And dirty. A dirty white shirt, a dirty white jacket (with a black stethoscope dangling from a pocket), dirty white pants, dirty (very dirty) white socks and dirty white—Maria could hardly believe her eyes—clogs. She'd never seen a doctor wearing clogs before. Although she thought it was kind of neat, she also wondered if there was something wrong with him. She shifted her gaze to the right to check out her mother's reaction. The word "hippy" practically flashed like a neon sign in Mrs. Tirone's eyes, but she said nothing. She just sat there smiling, her head tilted slightly to one side. The smile, tight and expectant, seemed a conscious effort on her mother's part to mask the look of fear and concern elsewhere in her face. Maria looked closely, cautiously. Was her mother afraid?

"So, Maria, you're eleven, hmm?"

"Yes, sir, Dr. Landra."

"And you have two brothers: Carlo, nineteen, and Joseph, thirteen. And a sister, Anna, nineteen months."

"Uh-huh."

"Your mother, Luisa, is a housewife. And your dad, Angelo—I guess that's where the 'Angelina' comes from, huh?"

"Yes, sir."

"—is a subway conductor. That must be a pretty interesting job."

"I guess so." To be honest, Maria had never thought much about whether her father's job was interesting or not. He never talked about it, after all, so she didn't know what to think.

Just then, another person in a white jacket came into the room. He was young, too, maybe even younger than Dr. Landra. Maria quickly checked out his feet. No clogs. Sandals. She wondered if doctors didn't get to wear regular shoes until they had seniority or something.

"Hey, Bob, how's it goin'?" The new arrival took in everyone at a glance as he slapped Bob lightly on the back. Dr. Landra lurched forward; his clipboard tumbled off its pudgy perch onto the bed. Annoyed, he started to say something, but the new guy beat him to it.

"Ciao, paisano, come si va?"[1] he said to Carlo.

[1] Hello, friend, how's it going?

[38]

"Uh, okay," Carlo replied, rising.

"*Ciao, piccerella,*"[1] he said to Maria then. Though she didn't understand him, Maria blushed.

"Your daughter, she's very pretty." His eyes twinkled as he spoke to Mrs. Tirone. She smiled openly in response, her fears seeming to vanish. Now, *this* was a doctor, a real TV doctor.

"I'm Tony Francotti. I'm from the Bronx. Where you folks from?"

"We have a house in Queens," Mrs. Tirone answered.

"Hey, hey, hey, a house in Queens. That's all right." Tony Francotti shook his hand in the air and nodded his head, a gesture that said, "Money, I'm impressed." Mrs. Tirone couldn't have asked for a better reaction; she loved telling people she owned a house.

"Dr. Francotti . . ." Maria's mother said then.

"Tony," Tony replied. Leaning forward, he almost whispered, "I'm not a doctor. Not yet, anyway. I'm a medical student."

"Oh, I understand," Mrs. Tirone said, her voice full of sympathy. For what, Maria wasn't sure. But maybe that explained the feet. Sandals must be for medical students.

"*Non devi aver preoccupazioni. Tonino e quì,*"[2] Tony said to Maria then, cupping her chin in his hands. She wished she knew what he was saying, but Italian was

[1] Hello, little one.
[2] You've got no worries. Tony is here.

her grandparents' language and a little bit her parents', not hers. Still, she felt safe with Tony. She was certain he was one person who would look out for her.

"Hey, Tony, do you mind?" Dr. Landra said, shaking his head. His voice was a little squeaky now, Maria noticed. "I'm taking a history here. Now, pay attention and maybe you'll learn something."

"Right. You're the doc," Tony shot back with a wicked smile and an easy wink at Maria. Suddenly, she didn't feel so safe. He seemed to be making fun of Dr. Landra. In a way, he reminded her of Bobby Truro, this kid in her class who was always goofing off. Sometimes Bobby was funny, it was true, and she laughed at the silly things he did. But there were other times he seemed kind of pathetic, like he did everything just to get attention. So you couldn't really take him seriously. Was Tony like Bobby Truro? She wasn't sure she'd want someone like that taking care of her. She wasn't sure she could trust someone like that.

"Now," Dr. Landra said after clearing his throat and lowering his voice to restore lost authority, "Maria has a VSD that was asymptomatic until recently. Maria?"

"Yes, sir?"

"When did your VSD start manifesting symptoms?"

"What?"

Tony jumped in. "Bob means when did you start feeling short of breath? Like after playing hard?"

"Tony, would you? Hmm? Please?"

"Oh, sorry, Bob. I'll be quiet."

"Thank you." Dr. Landra turned to Maria and cleared his throat again. She wondered if he needed a glass of water. "So, Maria, when did you start feeling short of breath after . . . um . . . exercising?"

"In gym class," Maria answered. "It was during volleyball last winter. I got really tired and had to stop playing in the middle of the game."

"Ah-ha. The winter, eh?" Dr. Landra nodded solemnly. He shifted his weight, and Maria thought of a jellyfish she had once poked with a stick at the beach. "And this was just about the same time the URI's started up."

Maria just shrugged. Why did doctors have to talk like this anyway? Would it be such a big deal if she understood what they were saying? She looked to Tony for a translation, but he was too busy reading over Dr. Landra's shoulder to notice her.

"Oh, wow," he said, his eyes lighting up. "A VSD. Hey, this is my first VSD. Great!"

Dr. Landra turned to Tony to confer on Maria's case. They talked as if she were no longer in the room.

"It's a pretty straightforward ventricular septal defect," Dr. Landra said. "Nothing fancy or unexpected. See, here are the results of the cath they did last month."

"Angiogram?"

"Right. You can see there are no surprises. It's a moderately large VSD located in the membranous portion of the ventricular septum, close to the bundle of HIS and below the aortic valve."

"Just where you'd expect to find it."

"Yep. Like I said, no surprises. It appears that there is sufficient pulmonary hypertension to warrant the recommendation of patch-closure surgery."

"Any hypertrophy of the heart chambers?"

"Nothing significant. But, of course, there's always the possibility of biventricular hypertrophy in cases like this."

"Really."

Dr. Landra and Tony turned to Maria and smiled. They weren't so much smiling at her as they were at themselves, at how much they knew.

Maria wanted to ask them to explain what they had just said, but she was afraid they'd answer in the same technical language. Then she'd be more confused than ever.

Tony winked at her (he was big on winking, Maria thought; maybe that would be his specialty when he grew up), and said, *"Non e problema, non ti preoccupare."*[1]

"Dr. . . . uh, Tony . . ." said Maria, "I don't understand Italian. Could you explain in English?"

"Sure," Tony replied. "It's no big thing is what I was saying. You got a little hole in your heart is all. Some of the blood's going the wrong way. Now, what we're going to do is—"

"—sew a patch over it, and you'll be as good as new," Dr. Landra continued.

[1] It's no problem, don't worry.

"Right. Better even."

Maria started to ask if that meant they weren't going to have to give her some dead person's heart, but a new voice stopped her.

"Landra, Francotti. Big powwow at the nurses' station. On the double."

"Okay, Wein, be right there," Tony answered.

Wein came into the room. She wore a dirty white uniform like Dr. Landra's. A stethoscope was draped around her neck, falling over her shoulders; her long black hair was tied back in a ponytail. Maria guessed that she was a doctor, too.

"Hi, kid, who are you?" Dr. Wein asked. She was direct, but not unfriendly.

"Maria."

"VSD," Tony added.

"Hi, Maria VSD." Dr. Wein extended her hand. Maria had never shaken hands with a woman before. It felt funny, but she liked it. "I'm Sarah VTI."

"What's VTI?" Maria asked.

Sarah Wein answered playfully, "Very Tired Intern."

"What's an intern?"

Dr. Landra said, "A doctor who's always very tired." He and Dr. Wein laughed, so Maria figured they must both be interns. She checked Dr. Wein's feet. Dirty white clogs. No question about it. There was something to this shoe theory of hers.

"Okay, Maria VSD," Sarah VTI said then, "I've got to take these so-called doctors from you for a big meeting. Don't worry, though, you'll see them again. They love hanging out with pretty girls."

Maria smiled.

As they left, Sarah introduced herself to Carlo and Mrs. Tirone. Then from the hallway, Maria heard her say, "Nice kid."

Sarah Wein's voice went on, "Oh, oh, here comes trouble with a capital *T*."

A moment later, "Trouble" poked her head in the door.

"Hi, I'm Linda," said the tall blonde girl in the Snoopy nightshirt. "I'm your roommate."

LINDA'S thick rubber thongs flapped noisily against the floor as she moved toward Maria's bed. She sat in the exact spot Dr. Landra had vacated moments before.

"You ever been here before?" she asked Maria.

"Just once, about a month ago. I had a cardiac catheterization done."

"Oh, so you were only in for a day or two. That hardly counts."

"How did you know how long I was in?"

"I know about cardiac caths. I know everything. Believe me, kid, I've been around."

Carlo laughed and said, "Seen it all, huh?"

Linda smiled in return. She had a pretty smile, Maria thought. "Yeah, you could say that." Then, with a nod toward Carlo, she asked Maria, "Is this your brother?"

"Mm-hmm."

"He looks like John Travolta," Linda said.

Oh, great, Maria thought, a new recruit for the Carlo Tirone see-him-and-swoon club.

Mrs. Tirone stood then. "Carlo, come, let's get some coffee downstairs. Maria and her new friend can get to know each other."

"Is that okay with you?" Carlo asked, rising. "We'll stay if you want us to."

"No, go ahead." At another time, she might have wanted her brother and mother to stay, but not now. She was curious about Linda; she wanted to find out what she meant about having "been around."

After Carlo and Mrs. Tirone left, Linda grabbed Maria by the hand and said, "Come on, I'll give you a tour. You can meet some of the other kids. Hey, what's your name, anyway?"

Maria told her as she slipped on her scuffies, which were lying on the floor by the bed.

"How old are you?" Linda asked.

"Eleven."

"Me, too. What're you in for?"

"I have a VSD, a hole in my heart," Maria answered.

"Yeah, I know what a VSD is. I knew another kid once who had one. 'Course, she was a lot younger than you."

"Oh, yeah?" Maria asked, but Linda didn't respond.

Slowly they walked down the hall, Maria peeking into the rooms they passed, trying to catch a glimpse of whoever was inside. Many were empty.

"What about you?" she asked Linda.

"What about me?"

"What are you in for?"

"Oh, cysts."

"What are they?"

"They're these growths I get inside me that have to be cut out. I've had a whole bunch removed."

"Yeah? You've been in the hospital before?"

"Sure, lots of times. I told you I've been around, didn't I?"

"And you've had operations?"

"Yeah," she answered with a shrug, "of course. A ton of them."

"Do they scare you?"

"Uh-uh. Sometimes, I vomit afterward, that's the only part I hate. Listen, you don't want to hear about my operations."

"Sure I do," Maria started to say, but Linda cut her off.

"Stay here," she said, "I'll be right back. I want you to meet somebody."

She disappeared suddenly into a room, returning a moment later with a girl in a wheelchair. The girl's leg was in a cast, extended out in front of her. As pale and blonde as Linda was, this girl's skin and hair were deep, deep black. The two girls looked like salt and pepper, Maria thought, but she kept the thought to herself.

"This is Bonnie. She's twelve," Linda said by way of introduction.

"Hi, I'm Maria."

"I know," Bonnie said in a husky voice that seemed much older than her years. "Linda told me. You got a hole in your heart, huh?"

"Yep."

Bonnie shook her head. "Tough luck. All I got is a dumb ol' broken leg."

"Oh, gee, is that all?" Linda quipped. "Would you feel better if I broke the other one for you?"

"Ha-ha," Bonnie said.

"How'd it happen?" asked Maria.

"I got hit by a car while I was ridin' my bike. Lucky for me the car was goin' pretty slow. Otherwise I might be pushin' up daisies instead of wheelin' around in this here Cadillac." Bonnie patted her wheelchair affectionately. "Pretty soon, I be up and walkin'. Mrs. Liebowitz, Judy—you meet her yet?"

"I don't think so," Maria answered. She'd met a lot of people that day and many of them hadn't told her their names, so she wasn't really sure.

"Well, she's the PT—physical therapist—and she says I'll be walkin' on crutches real soon."

"Uh-huh, and then the Lord help us all."

Maria looked up to see Miz Fielding walking by. She must have antenna ears, Maria thought.

"Mm-mm-mm," Miz Fielding muttered, shaking her head. "Get out the way, world, when this chile is up on crutches. She gotta lotta gettin' on to get on then, uh-uh-uh. Just you be watchin' out, world." She chuckled her way around a corner and out of sight.

Bonnie laughed. "That nurse is somethin' else."

"She's a real turkey, if you ask me," said Linda. "Always butting in with her opinion when nobody asked."

Maria joined in. "I call her 'Gotta Lotta,' " she said.

" 'Gotta Lotta!' " Linda said, laughing. "Why didn't we think of that?"

"Yeah," said Bonnie. "We've got names for just about everybody around here. But we never came up with one for Miz Fielding. 'Gotta Lotta,' huh? It's perfect."

"Listen," Linda whispered, "Miz Fielding—uh, Gotta Lotta—is nothing compared to Miss Sylvester. She's the head nurse, and—"

Bonnie interrupted. "We call her 'Hairy Terri.' "

" 'Cause her first name's Terri," Linda said.

"Is she hairy?" Maria asked.

"Uh-uh, but who cares?" Linda replied. "She's a real bitch."

Maria was surprised to hear Linda talk that way about a nurse. But Bonnie must have agreed because she just laughed her throaty laugh and said, "Ain't it the truth?"

They passed by a room then that was full of kids and toys and books and all sorts of things.

"This is the playroom," Linda announced. "It's a run place to go sometimes. The lady who runs it is pretty nice. Her name is Lorna, and she wears regular clothes and most of the time talks to you like you're a person."

"Instead of a germ under a microscope."

Maria peered through the window part of the door. A group of about five boys and girls were sitting around a large round table painting or making things with popsicle sticks and paste and glitter. One boy at the table was pounding on a big beanbag with a wooden mallet. A lady—Lorna, Maria figured—was leaning over him, talking.

"Who's that?" Maria asked, pointing at the boy.

"Oh, *him!*" Bonnie said with disdain. "That's Esvaldo. He doesn't speak any English. And he's . . ." She made a circular motion near her ear that Maria understood to mean crazy.

"Yeah, and he's real pushy. I just leave him alone," Linda added.

Then Bonnie started to laugh again. "We call him 'The Mad Bomber' because sometimes he gets so mad, he just unloads—you know, goes to the bathroom— wherever he is so the nurses'll have to clean it up."

"It's truly gross," Linda said, but then she laughed. "But it *is* pretty funny. Especially when it's Hairy Terri who has to do it."

"Wait, wait, wait," Bonnie uttered then with some urgency. "We're forgetting the best one of all!"

Monster Man! Come on, Maria, follow
p your voice down."

a wasn't sure what to expect as she followed
two girls down another hallway. Bonnie's wheelchair squeaked a little, and Linda shushed her as if
there were something she could do about it. They finally came to a door. It was closed.

"Damn," Linda said in a whisper. "I was hoping
you'd get to see him."

"Who?"

"Monster Man."

"Why do you call him that?"

Linda smirked, looking at Maria as if she'd just asked
the world's dumbest question. " 'Cause he looks like a
monster, what d'ya think?"

"Really?"

"Chile," Bonnie said, "you jes' keep away from Monster Man. He is mean, and he is ugh-*lee!*"

Linda motioned for them to move across the hall,
away from his door. Then, in a conspiratorial hush, she
said, "*I* heard that he is so mean his parents burned
down their house to try to *kill* him."

"What?" Maria asked.

"That's right. It was a long time ago," Bonnie con-
firmed. "That's how he got so ugly. From the fire. He's
been in and out of the hospital ever since trying to get
fixed. But, honey, when you're broken like that, you
ain't never gonna be fixed."

Linda shuddered. "Just the sight of him makes me

sick. He's all scars and . . . yuck, I can't even describe it without wanting to puke."

"He's a freak, that's what he is," said Bonnie.

Maria looked for a moment at the closed door. "It isn't his fault," she said softly.

"What'd you say?"

"Nothing. Just that it isn't his fault."

"Well, it's his fault for being a creep, though," Linda snorted.

"Is he a creep?" Maria asked. "Do you ever talk to him? What's he like?"

"Listen," Linda answered, "Monster Man doesn't talk to anybody. And nobody talks to him, get it? They even keep him in a room by himself. And that's just fine with me."

"He's gonna have an operation day after tomorrow," Bonnie added. "I heard the nurses talkin'. An operation on his skin! That is *so* disgustin'."

"I'm having my operation day after tomorrow, too," Maria said.

"We've had ours already," Bonnie said. "We'll be goin' home soon."

"What was it like?"

"What?"

"To have an operation. See, I never had one before. Does it hurt?"

"Not while they're doing it," Linda said. "Afterwards, it does."

"A lot?"

"You're not *scared,* are you?" Bonnie asked. Maria didn't answer right away.

" 'Cause there's nothin' to be scared of. Right, Linda?"

"Right. Like I said, you might puke afterwards, but that's not such a big deal."

"But what if—"

Linda cut her off with a look. "Don't worry so much," she admonished her. "Didn't anybody tell you there's nothing to worry about?"

"Yeah, everybody."

"So, believe 'em. Come on, let's go to the playroom. You want to come?"

"I guess so," Maria replied with little enthusiasm. She wished she could talk more about her operation, but it seemed like she was the only one who wanted to.

The three girls looked again at Monster Man's door in the hope that it would magically open before their eyes. When it didn't, they moved off in the direction of the playroom.

In silence they walked. Maria was bothered by their conversation. She didn't like thinking about the freak they called Monster Man any more than she did her operation. How could God let such a terrible thing happen anyway? Here was this kid who was probably just as normal as other kids, and then he was burned in a fire and from that day on he was different from everyone else.

What if God let something terrible like that happen to her? What if he made her different from everybody else? By the time she reached the playroom she was angry. And afraid.

FOUR

THE next morning, so many people were in and out of Maria's room she could hardly keep track of them all. She vaguely recalled Dr. Whelan waking her out of a deep sleep and telling her not to worry, that everything would be fine. At least she thought that's what he said. Everybody told her that these days, so it was a pretty sure bet he had, too. The rest of his visit, short as it was, she didn't remember at all.

Then another doctor came, a Dr. Hu or Wu. She couldn't remember exactly. He was Japanese or something, that's all she knew. He told her he was the doctor who gave the sleep medicine. He explained that she'd breathe in a special air that would make her drowsy. Then she'd fall asleep and not feel any pain during the operation.

"What if you run out of medicine in the middle?" she asked him. But he just chuckled and said that in all the years he'd been doing this, he'd never run out.

Gotta Lotta dropped in, too, a couple of times. And Hairy Terri. And Dr. Landra, who told her she was scheduled to go down to the x-ray department that afternoon.

"What do *they* want?" Maria asked.

"They're going to take your picture," Dr. Landra said. "Don't forget to smile."

Ha ha, she thought. Some joke.

Later in the morning, she had a visit from the physical therapist, Mrs. Liebowitz, who insisted Maria call her Judy.

"I prefer it, and it'll be easier for you to remember," she said with a smile so big and so white Maria thought she should do toothpaste commercials.

Judy explained to her that one of the most important things she'd have to do after surgery was coughing.

"Coughing?" Maria asked, surprised.

"That's right. It's very, very important that you cough deeply several times a day so that you keep your lungs clear. Otherwise, you could get sick. And you came to the hospital to get well, not sick, right?"

"Uh-huh."

"So you've got to cough, even though it will hurt. I'll remind you, don't worry. And I'll help. Okay?"

"Okay."

"Well, I guess that's about all for now," Judy said briskly. "I'll see you after your operation." And she headed toward the door.

There, she bumped into Tony Francotti, who whispered something in her ear. She laughed.

"You never give up, do you?" she said lightly as she walked off down the hall.

Tony entered the room with a smile and a shrug. "You can't blame a guy for trying, can you?" he said to Maria, who smiled shyly at him in return. She wasn't sure what he meant, but she had the feeling something sexy was going on between him and Judy.

Tony rattled on in Italian for a while, only one word of which she understood. *"Cara."* Cara means "dear," and Tony seemed to be saying it about her.

Then he said, "I have a surprise for you." From behind his back, as if he were a magician reaching into a black, silk hat, he produced a plant.

"Ta-da!"

It was kind of lopsided and very prickly. It was in fact one of the ugliest plants Maria had ever seen.

"Oh, it's neat, Tony. Thanks," she said, placing it on the windowsill. "I'm going to name it 'Cara the Cactus.' "

"What a nice plant."

Maria turned to see Lorna enter the room. Tall, with red hair and a ton of freckles, the playroom lady wore a gypsy skirt that swayed as she walked.

"Hi, Maria. How're you doing today?"

"Fine."

"Well, I'll be going," Tony said. "Leave you ladies alone. *Ciao,* Maria."

"Ciao, Tony."

Lorna watched Tony go. "He's a friendly guy, isn't he?" she said.

"Yeah," Maria replied. "He brought me this plant."

"I see."

"Do you really think it's nice?"

"I beg your pardon."

"You said when you came in, 'What a nice plant.' Do you really think so?"

Lorna looked at the plant and laughed. "Well, I guess the thought was nice," she said, "even if the plant is a little funny-looking."

"Yeah," Maria agreed.

"How are you getting along?" Lorna asked then. "You seemed a little upset when you were in the play-room yesterday."

"I'm okay."

"That's good. Have you had a busy morning?"

"Uh-huh. One person leaves, another one comes in."

"Has your surgeon been to see you yet?"

Maria thought for a minute. "I don't think so," she said.

"Do you have any questions about your operation? You're having open-heart, aren't you?"

Maria nodded. "I have one question," she said.

"What's that?"

"What's going to happen to me?"

Lorna smiled. "That's a pretty big question. Well, first of all, you won't be given anything to eat after midnight tonight. Then, first thing tomorrow morn ing, you'll get a shot to relax you."

"Getting a shot doesn't relax me."

"I know what you mean. But the medicine in the shot should help calm your nerves. Then, someone from the operating room will come with a stretcher-bed to take you down for surgery. After surgery, you'll be brought up to a special room here on the floor called the intensive care unit. You'll still be drugged so you'll probably be woozy, although you might feel some discomfort. You'll be hooked up to an IV to give you medicine and several other tubes for monitoring and helping you breathe. I can't tell you much about your operation itself, because I don't really know about it. You should ask Dr. Ohrne, your surgeon, to explain. Maybe you have some questions about it I can answer, though."

"Are they going to put some dead person's heart in me?" Maria asked.

Lorna's jaw dropped. "Wherever did you hear that?" she asked in amazement.

"Well, I have this friend . . ." Maria began, and she told her everything Marlene had said. Lorna kept shaking her head; and when Maria was done speaking, she assured her that when the operation was over, she'd still have her own heart.

"No heart transplant, I promise," she said. "What they're going to do is put a patch, like a Band-aid, over the hole in your heart."

I just hope it's a strong one, Maria thought after Lorna had left, because sometimes Band-aids fall off.

"Maria?"

Maria looked up. A short thin woman with wavy gray-blonde hair entered the room. Maria recognized her immediately. She had on a white jacket, but other than that wore regular clothes. Maria glanced at her feet. Tan pumps with a gold buckle. Normal shoes.

"I'm Dr. Ohrne," the woman said then. "Your surgeon. Remember me?"

Maria had visited Dr. Ohrne in her office a few weeks earlier. "Mm-hmm," she said.

She figured the doctor would sit at the end of her bed like everybody else did. But she didn't sit anywhere. Instead, she just stood there, her foot tapping lightly, nervously, on the floor, as she reached into her pocket and pulled out a clear plastic box with green capsules inside. She extended the box to Maria, who assumed the green things were pills of some kind. She wasn't sure what to do.

"Tic-Tac?" Dr. Ohrne asked.

Relieved, Maria smiled and shook her head. "No, thank you," she replied.

Dr. Ohrne popped a couple of Tic-Tacs into her mouth and stuck the box back into her pocket, at the same time extracting a stethoscope.

"Let's have a listen," she said, bending over Maria. She placed the cold metal end of the instrument first on her back, then on her chest. Dr. Ohrne didn't say another word the whole time she poked and probed and listened. But she made enough noise just sucking away on her Tic-Tacs. From the sound of it, this lady hadn't eaten in days.

"Okay, honey, you can lie back now," Dr. Ohrne said at last, tucking the stethoscope back into its precarious pouch. Maria didn't really feel like lying back just then, but Dr. Ohrne's no-nonsense approach didn't leave her much room for knowing her own mind. Obediently, she lay back against her pillow.

"There's nothing to worry about," Dr. Ohrne said. "I spoke to Dr. Whelan this morning. Everything's in order. You'll go down to the OR tomorrow around seven o'clock. The operation takes about four hours. By noon, you'll be up in the ICU. Then, you'll be on an IV for a couple of days."

OR . . . ICU . . . IV . . . It made about as much sense as alphabet soup.

"Okay, honey, I'll see you tomorrow morning," she went on. She was jotting some notes on a clipboard. Then, almost as an afterthought, she looked up and said, "Do you have any questions?"

"Well . . ."

Maria tried to think, but she was kind of confused now. She couldn't remember any of the stuff she'd wanted to ask. She saw Dr. Ohrne glance at her watch and thought she must have some more important patient waiting for her. Someone who was *really* sick.

"No. No, ma'am."

"Fine." Dr. Ohrne reached down and patted Maria's leg as if it were a dog, though not one she liked a whole lot. "Then, I'll see you tomorrow."

"Yes, ma'am."

And then, almost as if she'd never been there at all, Dr. Ohrne, the surgeon, the person who was going to cut her open and hold her heart in her hands, was gone.

THAT'S when her stomach started to hurt. It wasn't a real sharp pain like when she'd had the flu last fall. It was more a steady dull ache that felt as if everything inside her were slowly pulling in and staying in one knotted-up place. Like breathing in and never breathing out. Tight. Taut. Waiting.

She looked past the night table at Linda's empty bed.

"I *hate* staying in bed all day," Linda had said earlier. "It's so boring. Especially in the hospital. I'm going to the playroom. You want to come?"

"Yes," Maria had said then. But Dr. Landra had walked in just as they were leaving.

"I'll see you later," she'd told Linda.

"Okay. Later."

Well, it was later now—two hours later—and if Maria didn't go while she had the chance, she'd never get there. Quickly, before one more doctor or nurse could walk into her room, listen to her heart and tell her not to worry, she slid into her slippers and slipped out the door.

On her way down the hall, she passed the room belonging to the boy they called Monster Man. To her surprise, the door was open. She stopped and looked inside.

The boy was not alone. Lorna sat at the foot of his bed talking in a soft voice. Maria couldn't make out her words at first, but it didn't really matter since it was not Lorna she was curious about. She stared openly at the strange figure lying in the bed not fifteen feet from where she stood.

Faded brown pajamas and a white neck brace covered most of his body. What was really strange . . . and confusing . . . was that on his face he wore a mask.

Monster mask, Maria thought. Ugly! Why was he wearing it, anyway? No wonder all the kids called him Monster Man. If he was dumb enough to wear a mask like that, he deserved to be called names.

Maria looked at the mask closely. It covered his whole head. The first thing she noticed was that there was very little hair on it. What there was hung in loose clumps, as if somebody had hastily pasted it on. The mask's lower lip was swollen, puffy, distorted. On one cheek sat a long, shiny lump of . . . what? Silly putty, maybe. It was so different in texture from the rest that Maria wondered if it had been added as a last-minute touch. The eyes drooped slightly, as if they'd melted into position like wax that's dripped down the side of a candle. Why would anyone want to wear such a mask? she asked herself. Unless . . .

Suddenly, the mask lips parted and the boy spoke.

Loud and clear, his voice overflowed the room into the hall outside.

"I told you why, Lorna," he said adamantly. "They make fun of me and call me names. Have you heard the latest? 'Monster Man!' That's a fine one, isn't it?"

Lorna spoke up so that Maria could now hear her words. "No, it's not," she said. "It's an awful name. I won't argue with you about that. But I will disagree with your choice to stay holed up in your room. It's not good for you to keep to yourself the way you do. You need to be with other people sometimes."

"Why?"

"Because that's what living in the world is. Being with people. I know how hard it is—"

"No, you don't," the boy said. "You don't know because you haven't been inside my skin."

Lorna said nothing then. She looked down at her fingernails, absently picking at the chipped polish.

The boy shifted his position. Awkwardly, atop the stiff, ungiving neck brace, his head turned. His eyes caught Maria then, like the headlights of a car catching a rabbit. She couldn't move. She stood, sickened by the realization that the sad angry eyes piercing through her at that moment were not looking out from behind a mask at all. Not a monster mask. Not rubber. Not silly putty. But a real, human face.

"Why don't you take a picture? It'll last longer." His voice was sharp and accusing.

Lorna turned her head sharply toward the door. "Maria," she said, as Maria dropped her gaze to the floor, "were you looking for me?"

"She wasn't looking for you," the boy said. "She was looking *at* me."

"Now, Donald . . ."

Maria looked up at the mention of the boy's name. Donald caught her eyes with his own.

"So," he continued, "have you seen what you came to see? If you have, you can go. The show's over."

"I didn't mean to stare," Maria said. "I . . ."

"Come in," said Lorna. "I want you to meet some-one."

"Don't let her come in here," Donald said vehe-mently. "I don't want her in my room."

Maria stood transfixed on the threshold, but Lorna persevered.

"Come," she said, beckoning with her outstretched hand.

Maria stepped tentatively into the room. A wave of nausea rushed through her as she drew closer to the boy in the bed.

"Maria, this is Donald. Donald, I'd like you to meet Maria. Maria's having an operation tomorrow, Donald, just like you."

Donald snorted contemptuously. "Hardly just like me," he said.

"No, she's having a different kind of operation. And

she's never had surgery before. Maybe you can help her out."

Donald said nothing, just stared down at the whiteness of his bed.

"Perhaps Donald can answer some questions for you," Lorna went on. "He's been in the hospital before."

"I know," Maria said.

Donald quickly shot a look at her. "How do you know?" he asked.

"I . . . uh . . ."

"They were probably talking about me. They always do, Lorna. Talk, talk, talk behind my back."

"Linda was just telling me about the other kids here, that's all."

"Yeah, and I can just imagine what she had to say about me. 'Oh, did you see Monster Man? Ugh!' "

Lorna looked from Donald's angry face to Maria's chagrined expression. This was not going well, she thought. It was time to rescue them both. She stood.

"I have to be getting back to the playroom. How about coming with me?"

"Okay," Maria said.

"What about you, Donald? You want to come along?"

Donald regarded Lorna impatiently. "No," he said.

"All right. But please think about what I said before. Will you?"

Donald turned to the window, then back to Lorna.

"Okay," he said, "if you'll think about what I said. I have a right to my feelings, too, you know."

Lorna smiled with her eyes. "Yes, you do," she agreed, "and I would never take them away from you."

Maria glanced sideways at Donald as she left the room. "Bye," she said. He said nothing but, surprisingly, waved his hand in the air. It almost seemed a friendly gesture, and Maria wasn't sure what to make of it.

WHEN her family arrived to visit that evening, a huge arrangement of flowers preceded them through the door.

"For me?" Maria cried out.

"No, they're for me, silly," Carlo called from behind his parents. "And these are for me, too."

"Oh, Carlo!" Maria squealed as she beheld her brother coming into view. He carried a pile of boxes, all wrapped and tied with ribbons.

"Boy," Linda muttered under her breath from the next bed, "Christmas must be early this year."

"Sure, why not?" Mr. Tirone said. "For our Maria, Christmas come every day."

Not tomorrow, Maria thought.

"Where's Joey?" she asked.

Maria's mother raised her eyes to the heavens. "He's home watching Anna, *Dio aiutaci!*"[1] Everyone laughed as she crossed herself.

"Hello," a timid voice called out. Maria looked up

[1] God help us!

[66]

to see a small mousy-looking woman in a dreary gray raincoat standing at the door.

"Oh, hi, Mom," Linda called. "Come on in."

Linda's mother shuffled slowly, shyly to the far side of the room. She sat in a green armchair that was tucked into the corner.

Linda appeared uncomfortable with her mother's presence.

"Um, this is my mom, Mrs. Williams," she said in a vague sort of way.

Mrs. Williams acknowledged her introduction by dropping her chin and mumbling "hello" into her lap. Though she had the same fair hair and complexion as her daughter, she seemed as different from Linda as Maria could imagine two people to be.

The Tirones introduced themselves. Mrs. Williams nodded her head in response to each name, her hands pressing against her skirt the whole time.

"Don't let me interrupt the festivities," she said during an awkward pause. She nodded toward the stack of boxes on Maria's bed.

"Yeah, the presents," Linda called out, relieved to get the attention away from her mother. "Open the presents."

"Yeah, Maria, I'll let you open them," Carlo said, "even if they are for me."

"Oh, Carlo," Maria teased, pulling a frilly nightgown from the first box and holding it up for everyone to see, "you'll look so pretty in this."

Carlo blushed.

"Come on, Carlo, see if it fits. Try it on."

Her brother blushed some more. Maria could see that everyone was enjoying her joke. Linda was just about dying from laughter. Even Mrs. Williams laughed, though she did it without making a sound.

"Maria," Mr. Tirone said then, "open that one next. It's from me." A special present just from her father? That had never happened before, and Maria didn't know what to say. When she lifted the lid of the box and saw what lay inside, not only didn't she know what to say, she didn't know what to think. Swathed in layers of white tissue paper was a red satin heart-shaped pillow. It was trimmed with delicate lace. Maria lifted it slowly from the box.

"Oh, wow," Linda said. "That is so neat."

" 'Ts pretty," Mr. Tirone said. "I saw it, and I said to myself, 'That's for my Maria.' You like it, eh?"

"Oh, Daddy!" Maria exclaimed. "Of course I do. I love it." She gave her father a big hug and placed the pillow beside her. "I'll keep it on my bed always."

"Here," Carlo said, handing her another box, "this one's from Joey."

"From Joey? Maybe somebody else should open it. A mouse might jump out at me."

"Just because he did that once . . ." Carlo said.

"Did he really?" asked Linda.

When Maria nodded, Linda laughed. "That's great.

I'll have to remember that one. It'd make a great present for the head nurse, Hairy Ter—uh, Miss Sylvester."

"Oh, no!" Maria shrieked, opening the box. "He did it again."

Jumping from her bed, Linda ran over to look inside. "Oh, that is so neat," she said. "So neat" was obviously Linda's highest accolade.

Maria lifted out a gray, stuffed mouse. He had big teeth and a dopey smile, and Maria fell in love with him right away. Maybe Joey wasn't so bad after all.

"This is from me," Carlo said, pulling a tiny box from his pocket. Maria shook it next to her ear and said, "Is it a hot dog from Fisheye Freddy's?"

"Oh, darn, you guessed."

"Is it . . ."

"Come on, no fair guessing. Open it."

Maria removed the white box-top and saw, resting on a cloud of cotton, a small gold car.

"It's for your charm bracelet," explained Carlo, "until we get the real thing."

"The real thing?"

"Yeah. Our car. Yours and mine."

"Will it really be ours, Carlo?"

"Sure. I said so, didn't I?"

Maria heard a sigh. She looked over to see Linda gazing somewhat idiotically at her brother. She had that love-sick John Travolta-is-in-my-room-and-I-can't-live look in her eyes, which Maria knew required immediate medical attention. So she hit her on the head with a pillow.

The evening was perfect, except that it had to end. No one said anything about her operation until just before they were leaving, when Carlo asked how she was feeling. She just shrugged, as if having open-heart surgery were about the same as getting your hair cut.

"You're so brave," they all said.

"And you're *sure* you don't want me to stay with you?" her mother asked, as she had a few days earlier. "I still can if you want me to."

"No, Anna needs you at home. I'm okay."

"You're such a big girl," they murmured, rewarding her with smiles and loving touches on her cheeks and arms and leaving behind the presents that were the tokens of their affection and their guilt. Her mother cried as she pressed a rosary into her hands. Her father gave her a thumbs-up sign.

And Carlo, after kissing her on the top of her head, said, "Mom and Dad will be here in the morning. I'll come by after work. See you."

"Not if I see you first," she quipped.

And they were gone.

"Your mother seems nice," Maria said later to Linda in the dark.

There was a silence. Then Linda grunted, "Yeah, I guess. I like *your* family," she went on. "Everybody gets along so nice. I wish I had a brother like Carlo. I've been sick all my life, and I never had anybody on my side."

"I've been sick all my life, too," Maria said, but it seemed strange to say it. All her life she'd been sick, but she had never felt it. Not even now, really.

They were quiet for a long time. Maria could hear Linda's breathing becoming deeper and slower.

All of a sudden, she was frightened. Why had she let her mother go home? She didn't want to . . . she couldn't . . . pass this night alone.

"Linda?"

No answer.

"Linda, are you asleep?"

After a moment, Maria heard Linda's groggy response. "What? What is it?"

"Nothing, I just . . . Linda, I'm scared."

"Don't worry," Linda cooed. "Don't worry. Nothing to worry about . . . unless they make a mistake."

Maria sat up. "What?" she asked.

Linda mumbled something, but Maria couldn't understand her at all.

"Linda. Linda."

A slight wheezing sound convinced Maria that Linda had drifted back to sleep.

In the darkness, she felt for her slippers. Cautiously, she moved to the door and stepped outside. She headed for the nurses' station, hoping that someone was around to talk to. It was going to be a long night, and Maria wondered if she'd ever be able to sleep.

FIVE

THE night before surgery was always the worst, Donald knew. He stared at the telephone on his night table, wishing he could call Mother and Father Schultz again, just to hear their voices. But it was too late, they'd be asleep already. So, once again, he found himself alone.

He lay back against his pillow and thought about all the times and all the ways he felt alone in the world. Sometimes he felt alone even when he was with Mother and Father Schultz. And at school, well . . . at school he felt more alone than anywhere else. Surrounded by laughing, playing, normal-looking kids, he was isolated by his differentness. It was funny, but when he thought about it, the only place he didn't really feel alone was in his bedroom at home. His private kingdom, up the stairs, first door on the right.

He closed his eyes and saw the room clearly. The desk, orderly and neat, with its drawers arranged by category ("Art Supplies," "Writing Supplies," "Collections," "School Supplies," "Comic Books"), its top

Spartan-clean, just a globe, a dictionary and a blotter. Oh, and a snapshot of himself and his real mom that had been taken . . . when? He couldn't remember. When he was five, maybe. Sometimes, it was hard to believe that the kid in the photograph was him. Often, he studied that picture, the smiling freckled face under the mop of yellow hair, in the boy's hand a monkey on a string from a trip to the circus. It was the only snapshot he had of himself and his mother, the only proof that those two people really existed.

He had a worktable in the room, too, for his models. Mostly cars now. He used to do boats, and he had tried airplanes for a while, but he didn't really like them so much. Then someone had given him a model kit for a Camaro. He'd loved putting it together and painting it, even though he wasn't really good at the painting part. He enjoyed imagining himself the proud owner of the real thing.

His bookshelf was filled with books: the Hardy Boys, *Charlotte's Web* (his favorite, he'd read it eleven times since he was seven), *The Red Balloon,* lots of biographies of famous people and books about animals. On the top of the bookshelf was his rock collection and an autograph dog that was covered with the fading signatures of people he hadn't seen again and could barely remember.

The walls were covered, too, with pictures he'd torn from magazines, pennants and stickers he'd bought as souvenirs of this place and that and lined sheets of paper filled with writing. These were Donald's special wall hangings, some of the many poems he'd written over the years, the ones he dared to put up for all the world (Mother and Father Schultz) to see. There were others, of course; others that were for his eyes alone. They were hidden in the metal box with the combination lock kept under the bed or in one of the spiral notebooks that he almost always carried with him. Like his room, each notebook was a private place, a secret world that belonged to him alone.

Sometimes, he wrote things in his head first, then put them down in the notebook. That's what he'd done earlier today after Lorna and that girl had left his room. He'd started a poem about this new name of his, "Monster Man." He'd been called names before, but never this one. He wasn't sure how he felt about it, so he was writing a poem to find out.

As he reached to open the drawer of his night table, he glanced at the watch on his wrist. 12:30. It was tomorrow already. Today, no longer tomorrow, he was to have the operation. He'd had surgery before, of course. Many times. But it was never something he'd gotten used to. And no matter what the operation did, it was never enough. Today, for instance, the scars on his neck and left elbow would be opened up and expanded so that he'd be able to move his head and arm more easily. He'd stay in the hospital awhile, then go home still wearing braces on his neck and arm. He hated having to wear braces. They were such a damned nuisance.

The drawer slid open. He pulled out a notebook and pencil lying under a box of Kleenex. Switching on the overhead light, he turned to the last written-on page and began to read.

MONSTER MAN

Once they called me Spiderman
Because of the clothes I had to wear
the year after the fire.
Now they call me Monster Man
Because I wear my own skin
and the fire still burns on it.

Donald tapped his pencil lightly on the open page, wondering what the next line of the poem would be. A nursery rhyme came to him, one that had echoed inside his head many times since the fire five years earlier. Altering it slightly, as he always did, he chanted softly, "Monster Man, Monster Man, fly away home. Your house is on fire, and your children are gone." My house was on fire, Donald thought, and now the children are gone. Gone, whenever they see me.

Lost in thought, he didn't notice her at first. Standing in the hallway outside his door, Maria saw him, though, and wondered why he too was still awake at this hour.

When he looked up, she didn't move. They puzzled

over each other for a moment before either found the courage to speak.

"Hi," Maria said, her voice barely more than a whisper.

"Oh, it's you again."

"I was looking for a nurse."

Donald rested his notebook and pencil on his lap. "Well," he said, "there isn't one in here."

"I can't sleep. I tried to, but . . . I don't know, I just can't. Nobody's around. It's real quiet. Everybody's asleep."

"Except me," Donald said.

"Yeah, you and me. You're having your operation tomorrow morning, aren't you?"

"Mm-hmm."

"Me, too. I'm kind of nervous."

Donald said, "I hate operations. I hate everything about the hospital."

Maria heard movement somewhere nearby. At the far end of the hall she thought she saw a blur of white. She pressed forward, trying to balance herself on an imaginary line that was neither in nor out of the room.

"Are you scared?" she asked, looking at Donald again.

Donald considered the question, then answered simply, "Yes."

"You are, really? I am, too. What are you scared of?"

"All of it. Going to sleep, having them cut into me, not knowing if I'll wake up."

Maria took in Donald's words. "That scares me, too," she said softly. Then, to her surprise, she asked, "May I come in?"

"What for?" Donald was as surprised as she was.

"Just to talk."

Pondering her request, Donald placed the notebook and pencil back in their drawer. He turned back to the girl framed in the doorway and said, "Okay. But just for a minute. Shut the door behind you so the nurse doesn't see."

Maria readily complied.

"I think maybe I should turn out the light, too."

The room was flushed in darkness. Maria felt her heart beating rapidly in her chest.

"Do you think I could die, Donald?"

"I don't think you're going to, if that's what you mean," he said. "But that doesn't mean you can't be scared of it."

"Everybody keeps telling me I'm so brave. But I'm not. And I'm not a saint, either. I'm just me, and I'm scared something's going to go wrong. The doctors look at their watches and their clipboards all the time; it's almost as if I'm not there. What if they don't pay attention during the operation? They could make a mistake, right? Linda said they could. And what if they run out of sleep medicine, and I wake up and feel so much pain I die from it? My dad says not to let it hurt. As if I could help it."

"I hate it when people say that," said Donald.

"My mom tells me to believe in God, but how can I when God let this happen in the first place? Do you believe in God, Donald?"

"No," he said sharply.

"You don't?" Maria didn't know why she was surprised. After all, if she was having so much trouble trusting in God right now, why shouldn't he, with all that had happened to him?

"No," he said again, "but maybe I'm different from you. I haven't believed in him for a long time. It always seemed like he was on everyone else's side, not mine."

"What do you mean?"

"Like when my mom would punish me," he said, "she'd always say things like 'God hate you for a liar,' or 'God is going to get you for being so bad.' Then she'd hit me. Only I'd figure it was God doing the hitting through her hands. When the fire happened, I decided I must have been very, very bad, and God really did hate me to punish me so hard. It felt like he didn't believe in me, no matter what I did. So I stopped believing in him."

"Did your mom tell you God hated you, and that's why you were burned?"

"No, she just cried a lot when she saw me. And she never said anything about God again. Oh, except once I heard her tell a doctor that God must be punishing her. That's a good one. Punishing *her*. Like she's the one it happened to."

"What does she say now?"

Donald was silent for a few seconds. When he spoke his voice was tight. "I don't know. I don't see her."

"You don't see your own mom?"

"Uh-uh."

"How come?"

"I don't want to talk about that, okay?"

"Okay," Maria said. She stood in the darkness, as the unnatural quiet of the hospital at night enveloped her. After a moment, she spoke again.

"You've had lots of operations, haven't you?"

"Uh-huh," Donald answered softly. "See, when you've been burned real bad, you have to keep coming back to the hospital all the time to get fixed. To make it so you can use your body better. And so you'll . . . so you'll look better. At least, that's what they say. When you have burns like mine, 'better' is a stupid word."

Maria was glad the lights were off so she didn't have to see Donald while he talked about his looks.

"When this first happened to me," he went on, "I never thought I'd make it. Every day, I figured: this is it. I can't hurt this much and live."

"Did you think you were going to die?"

"Yes. And sometimes I wanted to."

"Really?" Maria felt her calf brush against the chair behind her. Without a sound, she sat down, keeping herself perched on the edge.

"The first time I thought I'd die was the fire. I tried to run, but there was no place to go. And then I heard this crashing sound, and I felt something fall on me, real hard. I thought the wall had caved in, and I *knew* I was going to die then. I couldn't breathe, I was being crushed. I think I must have screamed 'help!' or something, 'cause the next thing I knew somebody was saying, 'I'm trying.' That's when I figured out that it wasn't a wall on me but a person, and he was trying to crush the fire out of me. But he was crushing the breath out of me, too. In my head, I was crying 'Stop!' but I don't think I said it out loud then. I don't think I could.

"Later, after they took me to the hospital, I was shivering I was so cold. And I couldn't make sense of it, 'cause I'd been in a fire and now I was freezing cold. And I thought I was going to die all over again. But from the cold this time. In my head, I imagined I was frozen in a block of ice. I was screaming to get out, but stuck so I couldn't move. The ice made it so that no one could hear me and no one could get to me, but everyone could see me. They were all staring, looking through the ice at me. I thought I heard one of them say, 'Donald's frozen in the iceberg. Poor Donald.' And I shivered and I thought, 'I burned up. There's nothing left of me. How can I be frozen in the middle of this ice?'

"Then they started to chip the ice away. They took these picks and started chipping. And that was the next time I thought I was going to die. Each time they chipped that ice, they were chipping at me, tearing me apart. What the fire had left, they chipped away at until it felt like I was all gone. Until I was nothing.

"Day after day was like that. Sometimes not so bad. But sometimes just as bad or worse. And then one day I looked in a mirror and saw my face. I couldn't even cry. I just looked at this face in the mirror, and I knew then that what I'd been afraid of had really happened. I *had* died. The old Donald was dead. And this new one was here in his place. I had to get used to a whole new me.

"Now . . . this is the part that's strange, sort of . . . but I'm still afraid of dying. Even now, I'm afraid the new Donald will die."

"But you've had so many operations. Why are you still scared?"

"Listen, it makes sense to be scared. You'd be nuts not to be. Doctors are full of you-know-what. Nurses, too. They tell you not to worry. 'Everything will be all right,' they say. Sure, it's easy for them. They're going to cut you open and then go have lunch. What do they care? You're the one who's got to get through it. You're the one who doesn't know what's going to happen and just has to go along and say 'fine,' 'okay.' Stupid doctors! Sometimes, they never even told me I was going to be operated on. Just came to my room and took me away!"

"Did they tell you about tomorrow?"

"Yeah. They tried to, anyway. But I don't exactly trust them anymore. How can I? Just answer me that."

Knowing there was no answer, Maria said nothing.

"Anyway," Donald said, "you're not burned like me. What's wrong with you?"

"My heart," Maria replied. "It has a hole. They're going to patch it up."

The silence that followed puzzled her. Maybe her story wasn't good enough. It certainly wasn't as dramatic as Donald's. She thought of telling him she was going to have a dead person's heart put in her, but she knew it wasn't true.

Then Donald spoke, and she realized that she'd been wrong about his silence.

"I can understand why you're so scared," he said quietly. "Your heart is like life itself. Maria?"

"Yes?"

"It's okay to be scared."

She whispered, "What's it like to have an operation?"

Donald's words came out slowly then, evenly, each one considered carefully, weighed, measured, scrutinized for the amount of truth it contained before it could be entrusted to the air between his lips and Maria's ears. As if he were crafting a poem, Donald placed each word before his mind's eye, and then wrote it with his tongue.

"Your mouth is . . . dry. Like cotton. From the medicine they give you before you go into the operating room. To help you relax, they say. But all you want is to drink. And you can't because it's . . . not allowed. Nothing in your stomach before they cut. That way, if you get sick after, there's nothing to throw up. Even though sometimes you do anyway.

"When you get to the operating room, you're lying on your back looking up at these big lights that look like flying saucers from outer space. The doctors and nurses all wear masks and hats, so all you can see are their eyes. And it's like they're from outer space, too.

"Then they put a mask on you. But not like theirs. A rubber one, that fits over your nose and mouth. You smell sticky-sweet gas. It makes you want to fight. To push them all away. I don't want to go on your flying saucer. But it's too late now. You're tired. And you know it's no good because they're bigger than you, and there are more of them. And, anyway, you're the sick one. This is your part to play. So you don't run. You stay and you breathe in the sticky-sweet air. And soon, you fly off into space where you don't know anything anymore except the blackness.

"You don't dream. There are no colors. Only space. Night. But not a night with light and noises. A night without stars. That's what it's like. No stars. Just black, black, blackness. And it holds you. And becomes your only friend."

There was a long pause, during which Maria looked past Donald's bed to the world outside the window. She could see the moon and a few stars twinkling in the heavens. It was hard to imagine just how dark a night without stars might be.

"Crash." Donald's voice startled her. "Boom. You're awake. The saucer has landed. You're home. But you hurt, and the lights are so bright, and the noises are so loud. And no one leaves you alone. You wish you were back in space. Clatter, clatter, clatter. So much noise. You feel sick in your stomach. And still, you're thirsty. And the smells. Everything smells like yesterday's garbage. And maybe you throw up.

"But then you realize: hey, I made it. I'm alive. I'm not afraid of dying anymore. I'm alive."

Maria considered Donald's words. I'm alive, she thought. I've made it.

"You see," Donald said softly, "it's not an easy journey. But you'll come home. And you'll be okay."

Maria stood up. Tentatively, she reached her hand out until it bumped into something. It was Donald's arm. She heard his breathing. She felt him leave his arm where it was.

She'd never touched a boy like this. She wasn't sure what to do. She felt his skin, bumpy and uneven where the fire had transformed it, under the uncertain touch of her fingers. After a moment, she lifted her hand away.

"I feel better now," she said. "I think I'll be able to sleep."

"Me, too."

"Donald?"

"What?"

"I'm sorry about this afternoon. I didn't mean to stare at you. Honest."

Silence.

"I'm telling you the truth."

"Yes. Okay."

She crossed to the door. Before opening it, she said, "Good luck on your operation tomorrow."

"You, too."

"Goodnight. And thanks for talking to me."

"Yeah. Goodnight."

Maria opened the door a crack and peeked out. The coast was clear. She ran out without a backward glance.

Had she turned to look at the boy on the bed, she would have seen that he was crying. Not because he was afraid and not because he was alone. But because Maria had touched his arm. And he had let her.

SIX

E MPTINESS does not require the absence of all things; it requires only the absence of that which is most needed or desired, that which is most central to one's existence.

Luisa and Angelo Tirone sat in an empty room. Surrounded by the flowers, the games, the books, the cards taped to the walls, the water pitchers, the wash basins, the chairs, the slippers on the floor, the gray mouse and the red, satin heart, they had never been in so empty a place. The sheets on their daughter's bed lay as they were left earlier that morning, rumpled from her transfer to the stretcher-bed that had taken her to surgery.

Luisa sat in the green chair in the far corner on Linda's side of the room. She understood now why Mrs. Williams had retreated to it the night before. Tucked tightly into its nook between a dresser and the window-sill, it offered refuge to the world-wary. From this haven, it was possible to be in the room, yet remain apart from it.

The rosary beads falling familiarly through her

damp fingers, Luisa looked at her husband's back, slumped, as he sat on the edge of Maria's bed. He said nothing, just looked at his watch (10:30, 10:37, 10:41), stood, paced a few feet, returned to the bed and sat, his back muscles relaxing again to their unaccustomed slouch. He lifted his hand to his mouth, dug at a piece of imaginary food caught between his teeth, let his hand drop, looked at his watch (10:44).

"Hail Mary full of grace the Lord is with thee . . ."

Maria had gone to the operating room at seven o'clock. They had been told that surgery would take four to five hours, then their daughter would be brought directly to the intensive care unit on the floor. Until noon there was nothing to do but sit and wait, hoping that everything was going as it should.

"Blessed art thou among women and blessed is the fruit of thy womb, Jesus . . ."

Linda was gone, having left for Bonnie's room soon after the Tirones' arrival.

"I got nervous parents in my room. Can I hang out here till the playroom opens?"

"Sure. We can watch 'Sesame Street' and pretend we're kids again. Hey, guess what? I'm getting crutches today."

"Oh, Bonnie, that is so neat."

"Yeah, and pretty soon I'll be goin' home."

"Great! Me, too."

Angelo stared at the door. When is someone going to come in? he wondered. When are they going to tell me my little girl is all right?

"Hail Mary Mother of God pray for us sinners now and at the hour of our death. Amen."

He listened to Luisa's voice, letting the words fill his head. He was glad the church gave his wife such comfort. It just didn't work for him, that's all, no use pretending. Oh sure, when he was a child, being an altar boy made him feel good, real good. He laughed to himself, remembering the day he'd told his mother he'd decided to become a priest. She had wept for joy. *"Mio figlio Angelo—un prete!"*[1] In his honor, she made her special lasagna that night, and they drank wine and laughed and sang until very late. And everytime she looked up at him, fresh tears rimmed her eyes. But the next day, he changed his mind. He'd rather be a truck driver like his father, he decided. He never said anything to her, though. And as it turned out, he never had to, because she died of the cancer just a few years later, when he was fifteen. He remembered her face looking up at him, so full of pride. "Father Angelo," she said. "Maybe one day you be the pope." And he told her, "Yeah, Mama, who knows? Pope Angie the First, eh?" And she died believing his lies. While the truth he carried inside him like an unborn baby. It was better though, wasn't it? Better his mama should die happy,

[1] My son Angelo—a priest!

believing her son the truck driver would become a pope.

Angelo shook his head to clear the memories away. Why was he thinking of his mother now, of her dying, of his never-told truths and unspoken lies? He glanced at his watch. 11:03. Without thinking, he raised a hand to his mouth and picked at the space between his two front teeth.

At 11:37, Angelo looked up from his watch to the doorway. An excited commotion outside commanded his attention.

" 'Ts Maria," he uttered with absolute certainty. His sandpaper voice was that of someone who has not spoken for hours. Quickly, he rose from the bed and, joined by his wife, approached the door in time to observe a flurry of white uniforms whiz by. In the center of the flurry was a bed. The Tirones caught a glimpse of the pale, white child on the bloodstained sheet, attached to what looked like hundreds of tubes and wires and bottles.

"*Dio mio!*[1]" Luisa cried out weakly. Her knees felt as if they were going to buckle. "What have they done to her?"

Without a word, Angelo raced down the hall after the caravan. Before he could reach it, it disappeared through a door marked "Intensive Care Unit—Authorized Personnel Only."

"Mr. Tirone!"

[1] Oh, my God!

He turned back to see a nurse walking briskly toward him; his wife was at her side. Short and full of energy, the nurse was slightly out of breath when she reached him. He glanced at her nameplate—Kathy McGill—and the thought occurred to him that he had not seen her before.

"You can go in in a few minutes," she said right away. "Maria is doing fine. Dr. Ohrne is in with her now. She'll be out in a minute. They want to get your daughter settled before they let you see her. She's still heavily drugged, so she'll be groggy. Also, she may be uncomfortable and in some pain. Did they tell you what to expect?"

The Tirones' blank stares answered her question.

"This is often the hardest time for parents," she went on. Her hand touched Luisa's arm lightly as she spoke. "The last time you saw Maria she appeared healthy. Right now, she isn't looking so good. It can be quite a shock when you first see her. She may have black and blue marks from surgery. She has a tube running into her nose to deliver oxygen, and tubes coming from her chest. These are to make sure that the chest cavity and lungs drain properly. They'll be taken out in a day or two. The IV tubes deliver nutrition and medication. The other tubes and wires are to help us monitor her bodily functions. They're safety precautions, nothing more. Don't let them frighten you. Do you understand?"

"Mm," Angelo grunted.

"When can we see her?" asked Luisa, unable to think of anything else.

"In a moment, in just a moment."

The door to the intensive care unit burst open. Dr. Ohrne came right over to Maria's parents. She seemed exhausted and glowing at the same time, as if she'd just won an Olympic Gold Medal.

"Maria is in great shape!" she exclaimed enthusiastically. "The operation went fine. No complications, no problems. If everything goes well, she should have a normal recovery and in a week to ten days leave the hospital. By the time school starts, she'll be better than new. You'll see."

"Oh, thank you, doctor," Luisa said. Thank you, God. "May we see her now?"

"Yes, of course."

When Maria saw her mother coming toward her, she thought she was dreaming. Mommy, she cried in her dream-mind, I hurt. Everything was fuzzy, out-of-focus. And then, just before drifting off to sleep, one thought came to her with crystal clarity. Looking up at her mother and father standing over her bed, she thought, I made it. I'm alive.

MUCH of the next two days were a blur to Maria. Mostly, she remembered the pain and the coughing.

"Cough hard," Judy kept saying. "Harder. Harder. I know it hurts, but it's important. Very important."

And it did hurt. She felt like hitting Judy sometimes for making her hurt so much.

But it wasn't just pain she felt. She was achy and restless from having to lie in bed all the time. She wanted to get up and do things. But just the thought made her tired. And then she'd fall asleep. When she woke up, she'd be unsure where she was, what had happened to her, what time it was. There were no windows in the intensive care unit (she found out that's what ICU stands for), so there were times she couldn't even tell if it was day or night.

Her mother was there sometimes. And her father. And once, Carlo. Or maybe she dreamed he was there. She was in such a daze most of the time, she couldn't really be sure.

Being in a daze, her thoughts often became jumbled. She'd think one thing and say another. Or ask the same question she'd asked five minutes earlier. But one thought was clear through all the confusion:

"I'm alive."

At the end of two days, after all the tubes and wires had been disconnected, this thought, firmly implanted beyond the doctors' reach, stayed attached.

"WELL, chile," Gotta Lotta said, as she pushed Maria down the hall in her wheelchair, "you be lookin' jes' fine. Uh-huh. Nobody'd guess you just had a big operation."

"Do I have to keep using this wheelchair? I can walk, you know."

"Oh, I'm sure you can. But you're a little weak still. Another day or two in bed, and then you be up and around, no wheelchair at all, you'll see."

They came to Maria's room. She couldn't believe it, but after two days in the ICU, it was like coming home.

"Maria!" Linda shouted. "Bonnie, look who's here."

"Now, you hush, you devil, you," Gotta Lotta warned. "You'll get this little girl's heart all worked up with your screechin'."

"I am not screeching, Miz Fielding. Oh, I can help."

Gotta Lotta was maneuvering Maria from the wheelchair to the bed. "You can *not*," she said firmly, holding Linda off with one hand while supporting Maria with the other. Maria felt her weight collapse against the mattress. What a relief! She hadn't imagined it would make her so tired just to ride down the hall. Gotta Lotta was right: walking would have to wait.

A husky voice said, "Well, it's nice to see they gave my Cadillac to somebody with class. How you doin'?"

Maria rolled her head to the left. Bonnie was standing next to the bed.

"Bonnie, you're walking!" she exclaimed.

"Uh-huh," Bonnie said, breaking into a big grin. "With a little help from my friends." She acknowledged with a nod the crutches under her arms.

"These two be goin' home soon," Gotta Lotta said,

"and then we gonna close the hospital down and declare it a holiday."

Maria laughed.

"Now, seriously, chile, I gotta lotta things to do. I don't want you outa bed for the rest of the day without help. So you gotta widdle or anything, you buzz for one of the nurses, you hear?"

Maria tried hard not to crack up. "Yes, ma'am," she replied.

"You gotta widdle now?"

"No, ma'am."

"Good. I see you later then. You girls let her rest now, hear? Don't be jivin' her."

As soon as Gotta Lotta was out of the room, the three girls broke into hysterical laughter.

"Maybe we should change her name to 'Gotta Widdle'!" Bonnie said with a snort.

"That's better than Hairy Terri. She says 'void'!" remarked Linda.

"What?" Bonnie said. " 'Void'?"

"Yes," and then in a perfect imitation of Miss Sylvester, Linda said, " 'Did you void yet? Did you have a movement? Was it a soft movement or a firm movement?' "

"Oh, gross," Maria squealed, trying hard to catch her breath.

"And Kathy," Linda went on, "she's the new nurse. She's real nice, but she uses the technical name for everything. 'Urinate.' 'Defecate.' "

"That's not so bad. What about Landra?" Bonnie asked.

"Oh, Bobby-boy?"

"Yeah, he thinks he's bein' cute or cool or some fool thing. He calls it 'Numero uno' and 'Numero duo.' "

"Uno, duo, cha-cha-cha," Maria said then, and they all rocked with laughter. "Ow, ow! Oh, my stitches. Oh, it hurts," Maria cried. They all tried very hard for her sake to calm down. But it isn't easy to stop laughing when you're in a laughing mood.

Late in the afternoon, Maria's parents and Carlo came to visit. Maria told them all about "Uno duo cha-cha-cha," but Mr. and Mrs. Tirone didn't find it nearly as funny as Bonnie and Linda had.

"Did you really come to see me in the ICU?" Maria asked her brother a few minutes later.

"Of course I did. Don't you remember?" he replied.

"I wasn't sure. I thought maybe I'd dreamed it."

"I can think of better things to dream about than a visit from me," Carlo said.

From across the room, Linda commented with a sigh, "I can't."

Ignoring her, Maria said, "I'm glad you came, Carlo, even if I don't remember."

"Oh, I almost forgot," Mrs. Tirone said suddenly. "Joni and Tina asked us to bring this to you." She handed Maria a large rectangular box.

An envelope rested on top; Maria quickly tore it open. Inside was a homemade card that read, "Hurry

Up and Get Well Soon." Two construction-paper girls on roller skates pushed a third girl in a wheelchair.

"That's supposed to be me, I guess," Maria said, showing the card to Linda. She was pleased that her friends had thought of her. Even more than the game of Bombs Away! that accompanied the card, she liked the long letter telling her how much she was missed and giving her an up-to-the-minute bulletin from the home front.

"Marlene is more stuck-up than ever," it reported. "She keeps dropping sanitary napkins out of her bag and pretending she doesn't notice. She is so cool! (Sarcasum) Boy, she must want us to think she has her period thirty days a month! If you don't hear from her, it's because she's too busy looking at herself in the mirror."

Maria finished the letter with a sigh. She missed Joni and Tina and wondered how long it would be before she'd see them again. She hated to admit it, but she even missed crazy Marlene.

The time with her family went by, as it always did, too quickly. Soft goodbye kisses, and it was over.

As they were leaving, Maria asked her father, "While I was in the operating room, where were you?"

"Here. Waiting for you."

"Were you scared?"

"Scared?" Mr. Tirone seemed surprised at the thought. "No, no. I knew everything would be okay. I knew my Maria would be fine."

"I prayed for you," Mrs. Tirone added, patting her daughter gently on the cheek, "and God, he heard my prayers."

Soft goodbye kisses. *"Ciao,* Maria." *"Ciao,* Carlo." And it was over.

"Want to watch TV?" Linda asked later. " 'Danger Squad' is on. You ever see it?"

"A few times," Maria answered.

Linda flicked on the television set with the remote control lying on her bed.

"Now all we need is popcorn," she remarked.

"Yeah."

The girls watched for several minutes, when Linda said, "I saw this one already. It's stupid. That guy over there, the real dorky one?"

"Yeah?" Maria was trying to concentrate, but Linda liked to talk during television shows. It was one of her less endearing qualities.

"He murders the other guy's brother, 'cause the brother's trying to blackmail him 'cause he's pushing dope and having an affair with the other guy's wife, see, and the guy finds out and tells him unless he comes up with the money, he's going to tell his brother. And he can't come up with the money 'cause the mob is after him and he owes them money, too. But he gets caught anyway, so what's the difference?"

Maria gave Linda a long, hard look. "Thanks a bunch," she said. "You just saved me the trouble of watching it."

"Well, it's so *stupid*," Linda said, oblivious to Maria's displeasure. As she began switching channels with the remote control, she noticed a lone figure standing several feet outside the door.

"Oh, my god!" she said in a hushed tone. "Don't look now, but we have a visitor."

"Who?" Maria asked, without turning.

"I don't believe it."

"Who?" Maria insisted.

"M.M."

"Huh?" Slowly, Maria turned her head in the direction of the door. Donald, his left arm stretched out straight in a brace, stood looking into the room, a window-shopper afraid to enter because he has no money to buy.

"Hi, Maria," he said after a moment.

"Hi, Donald."

"I . . . um . . . I saw you going into the operating room. You were on a stretcher near mine. I guess you didn't see me."

"No."

"How are you feeling?"

"Okay. How about you?"

"Oh, not too bad. I didn't have to go to the ICU like you did. I went to the regular recovery room and then back to my room."

"You want to come in?"

Linda gasped. "Don't ask him in *here*," she pleaded in a whisper.

"No . . . I, uh . . . I just wanted to see how you were. 'Bye."

And, without a further word, he disappeared from sight.

" 'Bye," Maria said softly.

"Oh, my God," Linda mumbled. "The monster's out of his cage."

SEVEN

SETTLING into a chair too small for her long, lanky body, Lorna Barthels propped her feet up on the art table and reached for her cherished post-lunch cup of coffee. She relished these few minutes of quiet before the afternoon session began. Letting her gaze drift out the window over the tops of the neighboring buildings to the East River and beyond, she raised the cup to her lips and contemplated the morning just past.

Esvaldo's restless energy and relentless chattering in Spanish had tired her today. Was she getting old, she wondered, or was she worn down by the strain of trying to understand the ceaseless, urgent demands made upon her in a language not her own? It really was ridiculous, she told herself, that she'd never taken even an introductory course in Spanish, when for so many of the patients at DeWitte it was all they spoke or understood. She made a mental note, as she did at least two or three times a week, to check into evening classes.

She thought then of Tasha, whose silence was at times as deafening as Esvaldo's jabbering. Tasha, stationed before the easel, filled in her stained-glass window designs with colors rich and vibrant, celebrations of an inner joy known to her alone. Over the past weeks, Lorna had hung several of the paintings around the room, prompting one new arrival to exclaim, "Is this a playroom or a chapel?"

If the place were a chapel, then Bonnie and Linda were its choir. Lorna laughed to think of the contagious spirit these two so often brought with them to the playroom, their giggles bounding in the door before them. She was glad to see Bonnie getting around on crutches now, even as it made her think of those who would never be able to walk, with crutches or without.

Like Craig, who at seven, knew the world only from the vantage point of his wheelchair, who might one day grow tall but never taller. Craig once told her that his dream was to play baseball, like his older brother did, even if he had to slide into homeplate on wheels.

She wished that Donald showed some of Craig's determination to survive in a world with others. She'd tried so many times to introduce him to other children, to get him to join in group activities in the playroom. But every effort had been to no avail. Until . . .

She recalled seeing him walking down the hall with Maria that morning. Strange, she had never thought anything would come of their seemingly ill-fated meeting a few days earlier. Maria had been so timid, so frightened, when she first encountered Donald. Perhaps,

Lorna had concluded upon later reflection, she was just too young to be able to handle someone like Donald and his problems. And Donald hadn't exactly encouraged her friendship. Odd that they should now have been together. Maybe something good was in the wind. Unthinkingly, Lorna tapped the wooden surface of the table with her knuckles.

A rapping on the door echoed the sound. Lorna looked up at the clock. Two o'clock. The hour when meditation gives way to action. Hurriedly, she rinsed her coffee cup. The tapping on the door grew louder.

"Coming," she called as she dried her hands.

She opened the door.

"Well, knock me over with a feather. Look who's here."

"That's a funny way to say hello," Maria said as she entered the room. Her companion trailed shyly behind her. "I'm feeling better now."

"I'm glad. It's four days since your surgery, isn't it?"

"Mm-hmm. I'm tired of being in bed. The doctor told me I could come here if I played quietly."

Lorna smiled. "Then we'll find something quiet for you to do," she said. "Hello, Donald. It's nice to see you."

Donald wanted to drop his head, but the neck brace prevented it. The best he could do was lower his eyes.

"Maria said she wouldn't come unless I came with her," he muttered.

"I see," Lorna said. "You came for Maria's sake."

"Sort of."

"Well, whatever the reason, I'm happy you're both here. Why don't you sit down, and we'll find projects for you?"

Maria and Donald pulled out chairs next to each other at the table and sat down. Donald placed his braced left arm on the painted, wooden surface.

"This is a pretty table," Maria commented.

"Yes, isn't it?" Lorna agreed. "Several children painted the pictures on it a few years ago. Do you like to paint?"

"Yes," Maria answered quickly.

"No," Donald said at the very same moment.

Maria looked at Donald who kept his eyes down. Lorna cocked her head slightly as if to ask, "Well?"

"Not right now," Maria said.

"Okay. Let's see, then. How about macrame?"

Donald and Maria looked at each other and wrinkled their noses.

"No, huh? All right. What about . . . drawing? Clay?"

"Drawing!" Donald shot back.

"Clay!" said Maria.

Lorna laughed. "Look, there's no reason you have to do the same thing at the same time." She opened the supply closet and took out pencils and paper for Donald, a huge wad of clay for Maria.

"Maria," she said as she set the clay before her, "if you make something you want to keep, we'll let it harden and you can paint it later. Okay?"

"Okay." Maria looked eagerly at the clay, trying to imagine what she would make it become.

"Quitate del medio, gordiflona.[1]"

"A quien tu llamas gorda, cara de rana?[2]"

Carmen and Esvaldo exploded into the room. Carmen ran immediately to Lorna, throwing her arms around her waist.

"Lorna, that boy called me fat," she whined. "I'm *not* fat. Tell him, Lorna. Make him stop saying it."

Esvaldo stuck his tongue out at Carmen. *"Llorona, niñita llorona,[3]"* he chanted. Carmen started to whimper.

"Now look, you two," Lorna said, "why must you go at each other all the time? Come, let's see if we can find something nice and quiet for each of you to do by yourselves. Carmen, how about the sandbox?"

"No, I don't *want* to play in the sandbox," Carmen snapped.

"All right," Lorna said, glancing at the clock. 2:06. She sighed. "Let's go to the story corner and find a book to read."

Reluctantly, Carmen agreed to Lorna's plan. Lorna turned back to the two artists-in-residence at the table.

[1] Get out of my way, fatso.
[2] Who are you calling fat, frog-face?
[3] Cry baby, little baby.

"Do you two have everything you need?"

"Yes, thank you," Maria answered. She was glad Carmen would be on the other side of the room. Ever since she and Esvaldo had come in, Donald's eyes had looked like a puppy's after being hit: frightened and on-guard.

Lorna put her arm around Carmen's shoulders and steered her to the story corner. As they passed the sandbox, Esvaldo, who had apparently claimed it as his own, spilled some sand onto Carmen's foot.

"*Gordiflona,*[1]" he muttered.

"*Yo no soy gorda,*[2]" she declared, as Lorna's firm grip restrained her from hitting Esvaldo on the head with a sand shovel.

"*Dios, dame fuerza,*[3]" Lorna mumbled, surprised to discover that she did know some Spanish after all.

"HOW old are you?" Maria asked, twisting the clay into odd shapes, none of which inspired her imagination.

Donald kept his eyes on the paper before him. He was drawing a man—a cowboy, maybe, or an astronaut.

"Eleven," he answered.

Maria looked up. "I am, too," she said. "I'll be twelve soon. Where do you go to school?"

"In Brewster."

[1] Fatso.
[2] I am not fat.
[3] God give me strength.

"Where's that?"

"It's where I live. You never heard of it?"

"Uh-uh," Maria said. "Where is it?"

"North of here. Maybe an hour in the car."

"That's not so far. Is it nice?"

Donald shrugged. "Yeah, I guess so. What's 'nice' mean?"

"I don't know. Pretty."

Donald laughed. "I never thought of it as pretty. There's trees and stuff . . . and farms . . . if that's what you mean."

"Are there horses?"

"Some, yeah."

"Do you live in a house or an apartment?"

"A house."

"So do I. I live in Queens. You know where that is?"

"Of course I do. Everybody knows where Queens is."

"Not everybody. I didn't until three years ago. That's when we moved there. I go to P.S. 107. It's a good school, except I hate science and social studies. I like English best. I'm good in it, too."

"Me, too," Donald interjected.

"I used to like gym class. I mean it was okay, but then when I started having trouble with my heart and stuff, well, I didn't like it so much. You know?"

Donald stopped drawing and stared at the paper. The figure was not yet cowboy, not yet astronaut. It was like a mannequin in a store window, waiting to be dressed.

"Do you like gym?" Maria asked, deciding at that moment to form her clay into a horse.

Donald didn't answer her question. Instead, he flip-flopped his pencil across the sheet of paper before him so that heavy black lines gradually shrouded his astronaut/cowboy.

"What are you doing that for?" Maria asked.

"No reason." Donald crumpled the paper into a ball, pushing it to the center of the table. He began a second drawing.

Maria watched him out of the corner of her eye. She tried to make believe she'd never seen him before; she wanted to know if the sight of him would still make her feel sick. But it was too late, she was used to him already. She knew he was strange-looking, ugly even, but so what? He was different, that's all. Like her and her scar. Maybe. She wasn't sure how she felt about that one yet.

"What do you like?" she asked.

"What do you mean, what do I like?"

"Like I like roller-skating and the color pink and 'A Better Life,' and Groovy Monday, and peanut-butter fudge."

"What are those?"

"What?"

" 'A Better Life,' Groovy Monday, and peanut-butter fudge."

" 'A Better Life' is a soap opera, Groovy Monday is a

rock group, and peanut-butter fudge is fudge that's made with peanut-butter." She paused, and added, "Oh, and I like hamburgers cooked on a barbecue. With lots of ketchup. So, what do you like?"

Donald's new man was becoming an astronaut. Either that or a guy with an upside-down goldfish bowl on his head. He tapped his pencil lightly as he gave Maria's question serious consideration.

"Poems," he proclaimed at last.

"Poems?" Maria asked, somewhat surprised. "What kind of poems? Like 'Roses are red, violets are blue—' "

"Not kids' stuff like that," Donald retorted. "Real poems. Poems that don't even have to rhyme. I write poems, and they don't rhyme!"

"You write poems?" Maria put down her lump of clay (it looked more like a hot dog than a horse) and stared at Donald. "What about?"

Donald kept his eyes averted. "All sorts of things," he said. "Sometimes I write about nature. About the sun or the stars or the moon. Or I write about people. Or animals. Lots of times, I write about what I . . ." He mumbled the last word so that Maria couldn't make it out.

"What?" she said.

"What I feel," he repeated a little louder.

"You do?" Maria asked, impressed.

Donald's eyes met Maria's. She smiled, and he looked away.

Neither of them spoke for a moment. Then Donald

said, "I've never had peanut-butter fudge, so I don't know if I like it or not. But I like regular fudge."

"Do you like chocolate granola ripple ice cream?"

"I don't know. I never heard of it."

"It's real good. I wish we had some now. It sure would taste better than this hospital food."

"That's for sure."

Donald studied his drawing. Then, he said, "We don't have what'd you call it?"

"Chocolate granola ripple?"

"Yeah, we don't have it in Brewster."

"So, come to Queens," Maria said lightly.

Donald snorted. "Fat chance of that. I never get to go anywhere. Except the hospital, of course. I mustn't forget the hospital. 'How I Spent My Summer Vacation,' by Donald Harris. 'I went to the hospital.' I give the same report every year."

"Really?"

"Really."

"Last summer, we went to . . ." Maria started to tell Donald about her family's vacation on the New Jersey shore, but not wanting to make him feel bad, she stopped herself.

"Where?" Donald asked.

"Never mind. Hey, can you say this? 'I go by Blue Goose Bus.' "

Donald put down his pencil and stared at Maria. "What?"

" 'I go by Blue Goose Bus,' " Maria repeated, a little

faster this time. She smiled with the pleasure of not tripping over the words. "It's a tongue-twister," she said. "Come on, you try it."

"No."

"Come on."

"I can't say it."

"How do you know? You didn't try."

"I just know, that's all."

"Listen: 'I go by Blue Goose Bus.' There! I did it again. It's easy, see? If I can do it, so can you."

"No, I can't! I can't talk that fast. It's hard for me."

"So say it slower. Just try, come on."

Donald looked around the room. Lorna was reading softly to Carmen and some other kids in the corner. Esvaldo was busy dumping sand on the floor. Tasha sat at the easel painting. No one was paying any attention to him. Almost in a whisper, he spoke.

"I go by glue boose blus."

Donald's eyes flared as Maria giggled. "You're making fun of me!" he exclaimed.

"I am not," she insisted. "Part of the fun of tongue-twisters is how they get messed up. Try it again."

After a quick glance about the room, Donald took another stab at it. "I glo by goo bloose bus."

Maria bit her tongue to keep from laughing again. At that moment, the door to the playroom flew open. Bonnie and Linda burst in. They stopped dead in their tracks the moment they saw Maria and Donald together.

Linda whispered something in Bonnie's ear, and the two girls giggled.

Maria's glance passed from them to Donald to the clay in her hands. Donald looked down at the table.

Casually, Linda and Bonnie sauntered over.

"Hi," said Linda, leaning on the back of Maria's chair.

"Hi," Maria mumbled.

Donald said nothing. He felt hot and tense.

Bonnie, moving easily on her crutches, came to Maria's side. "Watcha makin'?" she asked.

"I don't know yet," Maria answered, a little embarrassed that after all her pushing and shaping the lump of clay still resembled nothing recognizable. She wished the two girls wouldn't stand so close.

"We wondered where you were," Linda said.

"I was here. I was . . . um, *we* were doing tongue-twisters."

Donald hunched up his shoulders and continued to stare down at the table.

"Oh, I love tongue-twisters," Linda said.

Maria looked up, her face brightening. "Can you do this one? 'I go by Blue Goose Bus.' "

Linda laughed. "Sure. 'I go by Blue Goose Bus.' " Her rapid-fire delivery was twice as fast as Maria's.

"Wow!" Maria exclaimed.

"What about this one?" Bonnie asked. " 'Any noise

annoys an oyster, but a noisy noise annoys an oyster most.' Now, you try it."

"Okay." Maria furrowed her brow in concentration. After a moment's thought, she came out with it, one word rolling neatly after the other.

"That's a good one," she said with a smile. Then, turning to Donald, she asked, "You want to try it?"

Donald stiffened. He could barely relax the muscles around his mouth enough to answer. "No!" he spat out after a moment.

"You almost had the last one," Maria said. "You can do it. It's easy, see? 'Any noise annoys an oyster, but a—' "

" 'See?' 'See?' 'See?' " Donald shouted, cutting her off.

"Donald . . ."

He rose from the table. " 'See?' 'See?' 'See?' " he cried again. And then, shoving Linda out of his path, he bolted from the room.

Maria started after him, her eyes wide with puzzlement. Lorna looked up from her book, but held back from interfering.

"Maria's got a boyfriend, Maria's got a boyfriend," Linda began to chant.

"I do *not*," Maria retorted angrily.

"Well, what do *you* call him then?" Bonnie asked.

Linda said, "I call him a jerk."

"I'll say. A real bummer."

"He isn't so bad," Maria said softly. "He's just . . ."

"Just what?"

"Just different."

"Different ain't the word for it," Bonnie said, leaning against the table. She let her crutches rest at her sides. "Honey, what you want to hang around with a freak like that for, I sure do not know. If you ask me, they took that hole out of your heart and put it in your head."

"Yeah, Maria, we saw you talking to Monster Man in the hall this morning. Yuck!"

"Well . . ." Maria let the word hang in the air.

Linda taunted, "Like I say, must be he's your boyfriend."

"He asked me if I'd come to the playroom with him, and I said yes. That doesn't make him my boyfriend."

"Whatever you say," Linda said with a knowing smile.

There was a long moment of silence in which Maria tried to figure out what she should do next. Like the lump of unformed clay lying beneath her right hand, her thoughts refused to form themselves into any shape that made sense or inspired her into action.

Bonnie cleared her throat and batted her eyelashes, forcing Maria to look up. In her huskiest voice, she asked, "Don't you notice anything different about us?"

Maria looked from Bonnie to Linda, who put her index finger to the top of her head and twirled like a ballerina in a jewelry box.

"You're dressed," Maria observed.

Linda stopped twirling. "Give that girl a prize!"

"I'd give you my crutches, honey, but I still need them."

"You're going home?" Maria asked.

"Yep! Both of us, sprung at the same time."

Bonnie said, "We're just waiting for our moms, then it's goodbye DeWitteless!"

Linda raised a corner of her mouth and said quietly and a little bitterly, "I hope this time it's for good."

"I hope so, too," Maria agreed. She felt herself soften toward her friends. She would miss them, even if they had been creepy about Donald. And maybe they hadn't been so creepy anyway. He sure didn't make it easy to be his friend.

She stood and said, "Well, so long, you guys."

"We're not leaving yet," said Linda.

"Oh, yes, you are," Bonnie said, with a nod toward the door.

All three girls looked over and saw a pale white figure standing silently in the open doorway. A half-smile was all the woman's lips could manage. Her hands hung as shapelessly in front of her worn gray raincoat as the limp pocketbook that cascaded from them.

"Hi, Mom," Linda said.

"Are you ready, dear?" Mrs. Williams inquired softly.

"Yeah."

Linda turned to Maria. "Take care of yourself," she

ordered. "Don't worry about that VSD now! The worst is over, right?"

"Right."

" 'Bye, Lorna."

Lorna crossed to Linda and kissed her on the top of her head, the very spot where she'd ballerina-twirled herself a moment ago.

"Goodbye, Linda. And good luck."

Maria noticed then that Bonnie's eyes were moist. Linda saw it, too.

"Come on, you dope," Linda said affectionately to her friend, "walk me to the elevator." Then, in a lower voice, she added, "And don't be such a sap. You're going home soon, too."

"I know," Bonnie replied, "but then we'll never see each other again."

As Maria watched Linda and Bonnie leave the playroom, she picked up the clay and squeezed it tightly in her hand.

DROPPING it onto the table, Maria began pounding the clay with her fist. When, a moment later, she sensed Lorna approaching, she avoided looking into her eyes.

"You seem upset," Lorna said softly. "What's the matter?"

Maria gritted her teeth and stared straight ahead.

"Maybe you're angry that Linda and Bonnie are leaving."

In spite of herself, Maria nodded. A tiny "mm-hmm" escaped her lips.

"Sometimes, people make friends and then lose them very soon after. That happens in the hospital all the time. It's hard when it happens to you, though, hmm?"

Maria's right hand continued to strike the shapeless clay. She was silent for a moment, taking in Lorna's words. Then, feeling her anger build, she said, "Yeah. And sometimes, it's hard just being friends with certain people in the first place."

"Like Donald?"

For the first time, Maria looked into Lorna's eyes. Her hand dropped onto the table.

"Yeah," she said. "No wonder nobody likes him. I was just trying to have fun with him, and he acted like . . . I don't know what. He's creepy, that's all I know."

"Well, you're right about one thing. It isn't easy being his friend."

"No."

"Especially when other people make fun of you because of it."

"Mm-hmm. I don't like that, Lorna."

"No one does. Donald doesn't like it when people make fun of him either."

"Is he my boyfriend?"

"Well, he is a boy and he is your friend. But, no, I don't think he's your boyfriend."

"Then why do Linda and Bonnie say he is?"

"Because they like to tease. And maybe because

they're uncomfortable that you have any kind of friend-ship with Donald. People who are like Donald, dis-figured as he is, make other people nervous and fright-ened. You felt that way when you first met him, do you remember?"

"Yes. But I don't feel that way now."

"Why? What's changed?"

"I got to know him, I guess. I like him. Well, most of the time, anyway. Why did he jump up like that and yell at me?"

"Because he could sense how uncomfortable Linda and Bonnie felt. He saw them whisper and giggle when they came into the room. He knew they were making fun of him, and he was waiting for you to join them."

"But I wouldn't . . ."

"It's not so easy to stand up to your friends and not join in that kind of thing. Donald has known very few people in his life who have stood up for him. He has no reason to believe that you will."

"I guess."

Lorna reached out and touched Maria's arm. She spoke quietly. "Why do you like him, Maria?"

"Why? Because . . . I just do. Because . . . be-cause of the way he talks."

"What way is that?"

"Well . . . he isn't afraid to say what he feels. And he tells the truth. Like, when he told me about having an operation . . ."

"Yes?"

"He told the truth. I mean, even if something's bad, he talks about it. He doesn't pretend bad things aren't there when they are."

"As if not talking about them means they don't exist?"

"Yeah."

"Is that what other people do?"

"Yeah. They say, 'Everything will be fine' or 'There's nothing to worry about.' Or they tell you to be a big girl or to . . . to believe in God. Or they just don't answer your questions at all. And then how are you supposed to know if there's something to be scared of or not?"

"What questions do you have that people didn't answer?"

Maria dropped her eyes again. How'd they get talking about this, anyway? "I don't know," she mumbled.

"Do you still have questions about your operation?" Lorna asked. "About what happened to you?"

"Yeah."

"Like what?"

"Like everything," she said. "How do I know what they put in my heart? Maybe this patch or Band-aid or whatever it is will fall out and get stuck in my bloodstream. Or maybe they didn't really fix it so good, and I'll be sick again. Or die or something. I can't ask Donald this stuff, 'cause how would he know? He told me what it feels like, but he can't tell me what it *is*. He's not a doctor."

"You have a lot of worries you're still carrying around with you," Lorna said, looking into Maria's eyes. "I had hoped Dr. Ohrne would explain everything to you, but . . . well, never mind. I've asked one of the nurses, Kathy, to talk with you. You know her, don't you?"

Maria nodded.

"She can explain things better than I can. Why don't you wait here, and I'll see if she can take the time to do it now."

Lorna left the room, returning a few minutes later with Kathy. Maria hadn't spent much time with Kathy since she'd just started working at the hospital a few days earlier, but she liked her a lot. She noticed that Kathy was carrying a large book.

"Hi, Maria, how's it going?" the nurse asked in her easy, friendly way.

Maria smiled and shrugged.

Sitting down next to her, Kathy placed the book on the table between them. Lorna stood nearby.

"Lorna tells me you're still pretty confused about what was wrong with your heart and what's happened to you. I'm going to try to explain things to you as best I can, okay?"

"I guess," Maria murmured. She didn't have much hope she'd ever understand.

Kathy opened the book to a picture of the human heart. Maria sat for a moment, taking it in.

"Well," she said, thinking of her father's gift, "it doesn't look much like a valentine, does it?"

"No, not much," Kathy agreed. "It's not as pretty. But it's a lot more interesting.

"Now, every heart has two sides. And each side has an upper part called an atrium, and a lower part called a ventricle."

"Mm-hmm."

"The four parts of the heart—the right atrium and right ventricle, the left atrium and left ventricle—work together as a pump, constantly contracting and expanding, to keep the blood moving through your body. The blood comes into the right atrium and passes into the right ventricle. From there, it's pumped out of the heart into the lungs where it gets rid of the carbon dioxide the body doesn't need and takes in the oxygen the body must have to survive."

"Sounds like breathing," Maria said.

"That's right," Kathy answered. "When you breathe in, you're taking oxygen into your lungs, which the blood then carries to the rest of the body. And when you breathe out, you're sending out carbon dioxide, which is a waste product the body is getting rid of.

"Now," Kathy said, "when the blood comes back from the lungs with its nice, fresh oxygen, it goes into the left atrium, and from there to the left ventricle and then out of the body."

"What does this have to do with what's wrong with me?" Maria asked.

"I was just getting to that," said Kathy. "You have a ventricular septal defect, sometimes called a VSD, for short. 'Ventricular' refers to the ventricles. There are two of them, right?"

"Yep. One on the left and one on the right."

" 'Septum' means partition or wall. In this case, 'septal' refers to the wall between the two ventricles. A 'defect' is an imperfection or weakness. So what you have is an imperfection, an opening in the wall between the ventricles, an opening where there shouldn't be one."

"Which is bad, huh?"

"It depends on how large the opening is. In your case, it wasn't so terribly large. But it did mean that some of the blood that had just come from the lungs and was now supposed to go to the body went across through the opening to the right side of the heart.

"When you had surgery, the doctors opened your chest cavity—they actually cut right along what is now your scar line—and stopped your heart from beating just long enough to sew a cloth patch over the opening."

"Like Raggedy Ann."

"Except that in time that patch will become a permanent part of your heart, as living tissue grows over it."

Maria thought for a moment about what Kathy was telling her. So she didn't have to worry about the patch going anywhere, since it would become part of her.

Now she understood why the doctors kept saying she'd be "better than new." Because where there had always been a hole, from the time she was born, now there wasn't one.

"And now my heart is normal, just like everybody else's," she said aloud.

"That's right," Kathy concurred. "And as soon as you have your strength back from surgery, you'll be active and healthy and full of life."

Life. There was one thing Maria didn't understand. "How could the doctors stop my heart?" she asked. "Wouldn't I die if my blood stopped moving around?"

"There's a wonderful machine called a heart-lung machine—well, it's also called a cardiopulmonary by-pass—but heart-lung machine is easier. What it does is take over for your heart, so that your heart will be still and the doctors can operate on it."

"So all my blood goes through this machine instead of my heart?"

"Yes. And when the doctors finished sewing the patch on your heart, they started your heart up again, moving your blood through it instead of the machine."

There was a long moment of silence. "Wow." Maria said at last. "That is so neat."

"It sure is." Kathy laughed.

Lorna laughed, too. It was the first sound she'd made since Kathy had sat down with Maria. "This has been a lot for you to take in at one time," she said. "If you have any questions later, I'm sure Kathy will be happy to talk with you some more."

Maria looked at Kathy who nodded. "I sure will," the nurse said.

"I think I understand now," Maria replied.

"I'm glad."

Lorna asked, "Are you feeling any better?"

"Yeah. But what I *don't* understand is why people can't just tell you things. You know, simple, like you just did."

Lorna and Kathy exchanged a glance. "I don't know," Kathy said, raising her eyebrows. "Sometimes, the simplest things are the hardest, I guess."

"I guess."

Lorna walked over to Maria and put her hands on her shoulders. "What do you want to do now?" she asked.

Maria regarded the flattened lump of clay. It looked like an old pancake. "I know," she said suddenly. "I'll make a heart. My heart!"

"Terrific," Lorna said.

Kathy stood, reaching for the book as she did. "That's a wonderful idea," she said to Maria. She reached out and touched her hand. "I'm glad we talked. I've got to get going, but remember, if you want to talk some more, Maria, I'll be around."

"Kathy?"

"Yes?"

"Could you leave the picture? I want to make a real heart, not a valentine one. A real one with real parts."

Kathy smiled. "Sure," she said, pushing the book toward Maria. To Lorna she said, "I'll pick it up later. See you, Maria."

"See you, Kathy."

After Kathy left, Maria studied the picture carefully. "Hmm, let's see, this is going to be hard. First, I'll need a piece of cloth."

"A piece of cloth? What for?"

"For the patch, of course! This is my heart, after all."

"Of course," Lorna agreed, rummaging through a box nearby that contained scraps of material.

"And Lorna?"

"Yes?"

"Could it be a blue one, please? That's my favorite color."

Lorna held up a piece of robin's egg blue felt.

"How's this?" she asked.

Maria smiled. It was perfect.

EIGHT

"WHAT are you watching?" Maria asked Donald. She did not wait for an invitation, but sat down in the chair next to his bed. Donald had kept his gaze firmly affixed to the television set suspended in the corner of his room ever since Maria had come in. He had not said a word, not even "hello." When he did speak, it was more a croak than an answer.

" 'The Brady Bunch,' " he mumbled.

"Oh, yeah. Is it a good one?"

"It's okay."

Maria tried watching the program with him, but she wasn't really interested. She'd bet that he wasn't either; he had that glazed look on his face you get when you're watching television because you feel like there's nothing else to do.

"I missed 'A Better Life' again today," Maria said then. "I got so busy in the playroom I didn't think about anything else, and then Lorna said it was closing time. I couldn't believe it. I'd been working on my project for almost two hours. But at least I finished it. I made something out of clay." She wanted him to ask what it was, but he didn't ask anything.

"It's too bad you left in such a hurry," Maria went on. With the remote control switch, Donald turned up the volume on the television set. That's when she noticed the spiral notebook lying on his lap.

"What's that?" she asked.

Donald glanced down. Protectively, his hand fell over the notebook. "Nothing," he said.

"It is too something. You had it in your lap the night before our operations, too. Come on, what is it? Is that where you write your poems?"

For the first time, Donald looked at Maria. "You and your stupid tongue-twisters," he spat out angrily. Then he moved the notebook to the table on the other side of the bed, the side away from Maria.

"Are you still mad about that? It's no big deal that you couldn't say a few tongue-twisters, you know."

"Yeah, and you and your friends could say them all just perfect! So who looks like the stupid one, huh? Just tell me that. Who looks stupid?"

Maria said, "I don't think you're stupid, Donald. I never thought that. I think you're one of the smartest people I ever met." She paused for a moment. "I'm sorry," she said then, "if I made you feel that way. I didn't mean to, honest. Cross my heart and hope to—"

A commercial came on, and Donald flicked the image off the screen. They sat for a long moment in silence. Finally he said, "Okay. So what do you want to do now?"

"I want to read one of your poems," Maria answered.

Donald looked at her, surprised. He'd never shown the notebook poems to anyone except Lorna and his teacher last year. They'd liked them a lot, but that didn't count. They were grown-ups. It wasn't as if either of them was a friend. Donald reached over with his unbraced arm and resettled the notebook on his lap.

"Why do you want to read them?" he asked.

"Just because."

"You won't laugh?"

"Uh-uh. Why should I?"

Donald considered, then opened the book. As the pages fell through his fingers, he said to Maria, "Just one, though. Don't read the others. Just the one I let you read, okay?"

"Okay."

Maria felt her excitement growing. When he handed her the open notebook, she beheld the handwriting on the page as if it were a buried treasure that had surfaced for her eyes alone. A buried treasure from deep inside Donald.

"This is one I wrote a long time ago," he said.

"Does it have a name?"

"I call it 'A Dream.' "

Maria looked at the page and read.

*　*　*

My mother sits at the foot of my night-time bed,
The darkness holding her as her sweet summer song
　holds me.
Her melodious notes float through the air.
Her fingertips run up and down my leg.
And I say, "Mother, Mother."
She stops her singing and smiles down at me.
"Don't be afraid," she says. "Nothing will harm you."
And she sings some more,
Her fingertips resting gently now,
Letting me know that I am safe.
　And then I wake up.

Maria read the poem through twice. "This is sad," she said, after reflecting for a moment. She didn't really understand why it was called "A Dream." "Is it true?"

Donald's answer was not exactly an answer. "It's a poem," he said, "I made it up."

"Really?"

"Of course. Do you like it?"

"Oh, yes. It reminds me of my mother, the way she sings to me at home sometimes when I can't sleep. I guess your mother did that, too. It's just hard to believe you made it up out of your own head. It seems so real."

Donald was pleased. "Do you want to read some others?" he asked, his shyness suddenly gone. And then, without waiting for a reply, he took the notebook from her and selected two more for her to read.

Maria read them slowly. One didn't make too much sense to her, so she read it through a few times. The other was easier. It was about an old man in a hospital wheelchair waiting for his daughter to visit. But she never comes.

"I like them a lot," she said wistfully, "but they all make me sad." She handed the notebook back to Donald. She was glad he had shared his buried treasures with her, but she wished the poems, at least one of them, hadn't made her feel so sad.

"Don't you ever write happy poems?" Maria asked.

"I write the way I feel," Donald replied simply.

"Oh." For a moment, Maria gazed at the notebook lying on Donald's lap. Then she looked up at his face.

"Want to go to my room now?" she asked. "I have some neat games we could play."

"Maybe," Donald replied, as he put the notebook safely away in its drawer. "Yeah, okay."

"Did you ever play Bombs Away!? It's a good game."

"No, I don't think so. Do I need to use both hands?"

"No."

"Good. Will you teach me?"

"Sure."

Just as they were leaving Donald's room, he stopped Maria and said, "Listen to this."

Maria watched as his droopy eyes took on a look of

intense concentration. Then slowly, but with absolute assurance, the words came forth.

" 'I go by Blue Goose Bus.' "

Maria broke into laughter. "Perfect!" she exclaimed.

"I've been saying it over and over in my head all afternoon," Donald confessed. "Next time, I'll say it faster. Maybe even faster than you."

"COME ON, slowpoke, your move," Donald said. Nervously, he bounced the heels of his feet up and down on the floor, waiting for Maria's man to fall into his trap.

Maria pondered the alternatives carefully. If she moved her red forward, he would capture it. On the other hand, if she retreated, he would move in and take her green. Donald waved his right hand in the air.

"Come on, come on, come on," he chanted happily through gritted teeth.

"Okay, okay," Maria said, sliding her blue forward a space.

"Kaboom!" Donald shouted in glee. "That's a bomb! Gotcha." Merrily, he removed Maria's blue from the board. "Just a few more turns, and I'll win!"

Maria shook her head. "Are you sure you never played this game before?" she asked.

"Never," he answered crisply, as he moved a red one space to the side. "Come on, your turn."

Without thinking, Maria slid a green forward.

"Kaboom!" Donald screamed again. "Bombs away!

Didn't you remember I had a bomb there, Maria? Tsk, tsk, tsk. You're not paying attention."

Maria groaned.

"What's all the noise about?"

Maria and Donald turned to see a familiar face at the door. *"Ciao, bambolina, che si dice?*[1]*"*

"Hi, Tony," Maria called. "Donald's beating me at Bombs Away! That's what all the noise is about."

"Oh, yeah?" Tony came into the room a step. "Good to see you out of your room, Donald. And playing a game, too. That's pretty good."

"Yeah, yeah," Donald muttered.

"Hey, Maria, how's my plant? Doin' okay?" Tony crossed the room and crooned to Cara the Cactus in Italian. Maria giggled as Donald made a face that said, "Boy, is he nuts."

"Well, I gotta run. Oh, Maria, I think maybe I saw your *madre*[2] and *padre*[3] in the lobby a few minutes ago. With two guys. Your brother, Carlo, I guess, and . . . hey, you got two brothers?"

"Yeah. Joey. But he never came before."

"Yeah, well, maybe he came this time. See youse two, eh? And, Donald, go easy on her, will you? *Ciao.*"

"Yeah, yeah," Donald mumbled again.

"Gee," Maria said as she watched Donald move his green toward her red, "I wonder if it's really them."

[1] Hello, little doll, what do you say?
[2] mother
[3] father

"Your turn," said Donald. "Boy, that Tony is such a pain. 'Good to see you out of your room, Donald.' What's everybody making such a big deal for?"

"Nobody's making such a big deal except you," Maria replied. "And you could be nice once in a while. You don't always have to be such a tough guy."

"Who's a tough guy?"

"You. 'Yeah, yeah,'" she muttered in imitation of Donald. "You could say, 'Hi,' you know. It wouldn't hurt." She moved her red up and captured his blue. "Ha, ha," she said. "Gotcha."

"Beginner's luck," Donald replied. "Just watch out."

The two players settled down to serious business, and in the next few moves, Donald captured Maria's fortress and won the game.

"Victory!" he cried triumphantly.

"Beginner's luck!" Maria said with half a smile.

Just as they were about to start a new game, Maria's family arrived. Tony had been right.

"We brought you a surprise visitor!" Mrs. Tirone called from the doorway. She pushed Joey into the room. The rest of the family stepped in behind him.

"Hi," he said awkwardly. His discomfort at being in the hospital was obvious, made all the more so when he saw Donald. Stunned by what he saw, he wanted to turn and run. It was a feeling shared by Donald.

"I've got to go," Donald whispered to Maria.

"No, you don't," she replied firmly. "I want you to meet my family."

"But, Maria . . ."

"No." Then, looking her brother squarely in the eye, she said, "Joey, this is my friend, Donald."

Joey wished he could look anywhere but at Donald's face. He wondered what Carlo and his parents were thinking. He knew coming to the hospital would be gross, but he never imagined that it could be *this* gross.

"Hi," was all he said.

"Hi," Donald mumbled, averting his eyes to avoid all the unasked questions in Joey's eyes.

"And these are my mom and dad and my brother Carlo."

"Hello, Donald," Mrs. Tirone said a little uneasily.

"Hey, Donald, how ya' doin'?" Carlo said. He extended his hand. Donald gently laid his own in it. He started to say, "Yeah, yeah."

But instead, he replied, "Hi."

No one else spoke again for what seemed a very long time until Mrs. Tirone said, "You can't very well call me 'Maria's mom.' I'm Mrs. Tirone."

"Hello, Mrs. Tirone," Donald said in response. He realized he'd never heard Maria's last name before.

Mr. Tirone cleared his throat. "So, Maria," he said, protruding his lower lip, and scanning her with his eyes, "let's see how you look. Good, eh? You see, Joey, you see how good your sister looks?"

"Yeah, Dad," Joey grumbled.

"You are lookin' good," Carlo said. "How are you feeling?"

"Okay. See how straight I'm standing?"

Carlo nodded.

"Judy told me I was bending over because I was afraid of hurting myself. So she gave me exercises and stuff to straighten up. And now look how good I'm standing."

"I see, I see," said Mrs. Tirone. Maria noticed that her mother still had that worried look on her face, as if she weren't sure the operation had been such a good idea. The rosary beads were still clicking away inside her head.

"I learned all about my operation today," she said. "You want to hear about it?"

"No, no," her father replied quickly. "You don't want to have to go through all that again."

"That's right," cooed her mother. "Poor Maria. You've suffered enough. Anyway, we know all about your operation."

"I don't," Joey said suddenly, lowering himself into the chair in the corner.

"Neither do I," echoed Carlo. He sat on the empty bed. "I'd really like to hear Maria explain it."

Maria looked at Donald. He shrugged his shoulders. "Me, too, I guess," he said softly.

"Okay," she chirped. Pulling herself onto her bed, she crossed her legs and settled into a comfortable story-telling position.

Mr. and Mrs. Tirone glanced uneasily at each other.

"Well," Maria began, "the heart is like a pump, see.

It keeps the blood moving through your body, making sure it gets all the food and oxygen it's supposed to have . . ." And on she went, energetically telling them all about the lungs and the ventricles and the opening in the wall between her left and right ventricles and the patch on the wall and how that patch would become a real part of her and how she was better now than when she was a newborn baby even. And then she told them all about the heart-lung machine and how it made it possible for the doctors to actually stop her heart and keep her blood moving along.

"Far out!" Joey said.

They all laughed, and Maria said, "That's what I thought, too."

To her surprise, once she'd started talking, her family was really interested. Instead of, "Oh, don't talk about *that*," or "Let's change the subject," they said, "Really?" and "Then what?" and "I didn't know that. Maria, you're so smart." They really wanted to know. Even her mom and dad.

When it was time for dinner, Carlo said, "No hospital food tonight!" He and Joey went out and came back twenty minutes later with buckets of Kentucky Fried Chicken, a ton of cole slaw and French fries, cans of soda and iced tea.

Donald said, "Gee, all we need now is chocolate granola ripple." He and Maria laughed at their private joke.

And it was like having a picnic indoors.

". . . SO the man says, 'I was talking to the duck!' "

"Oh, no, Carlo, that's terrible!" Mrs. Tirone exclaimed, but everyone laughed just the same, Maria hardest of all.

"Watch out," cried Carlo, his eyes bright with the evening's pleasures, "you'll pop your stitches if you keep that up."

"Not fair!" Maria shouted. "You're saying that to make me laugh more."

Empty fried chicken cartons lay scattered, abandoned like litter on a post-holiday beach. Propped up against the headboard of her bed, Maria hugged her daddy-heart to her chest. Donald, sitting in a chair nearby, betrayed his sad eyes with a bubbling joy that surfaced and resurfaced with each new joke, waves happily lapping the sand.

"More!" Maria cried then. "Carlo, tell another."

"Tell the one about . . ." Joey started to say. Then, running to his brother's side, he whispered in his ear.

"Joey!" Carlo said in mock-amazement. "I can't tell that one here."

"Come on, bro," Joey replied. "Maria's old enough. Hey, come on."

"Yeah, but what about Mom?"

"Is this a dirty joke?" Mrs. Tirone asked, all innocence. "No, no, it can't be. My Carlo, he doesn't tell dirty jokes."

Maria could see the twinkle in her mother's eye. She

knew she was teasing Carlo, challenging him to tell the joke.

Carlo gave in. "Well, okay," he said. "Mom says it's not dirty, so I guess it's all right . . ."

Suddenly, Mr. Tirone became nervous. "Now, wait a minute, Carlo," he said, moving a step in his sons' direction. "Maybe you shouldn't tell it. Maybe it's better . . ." with a nod toward Maria ". . . she not hear."

"Tell us, tell us, tell us," chanted Maria, afraid Carlo would listen to their father.

"Come on," whined Joey, "what's the big deal?"

"Yeah, tell us, tell us," repeated Maria.

"Tell us," Donald echoed softly.

"Okay, okay." Carlo extended his hands in pontifical fashion. "Silence."

Everyone became very still.

"It seems there was this nearsighted snake, see, who was . . . um, in the mood for love. So he attacked a garden hose. After a few seconds, he stopped, wiped his mouth, and said, 'Boy, did anyone ever tell you you're a sloppy kisser?'"

"Oh, no," Mrs. Tirone protested between laughs, "that's awful. Awful, awful, Carlo. 'Ts awful."

"But 'ts not so dirty," her husband said.

"Of course not," Carlo said. "Do you think I'd tell Joey a really dirty joke?"

The laughter died down. Or most of it, anyway. As the Tirone family became quiet, Donald kept right on chuckling. He couldn't contain himself.

"Funny, eh, Donald?" Carlo asked.

Nodding stiffly atop his neck brace, Donald laughed some more. The sound of it built and built until the chuckle burst into full song, and the laughter rang. Soon, Maria was laughing again, too. And then Joey. And Carlo. Mr. and Mrs. Tirone joined in. No longer at the joke. And not at Donald. But at laughter itself. At the wonderful, silly, full-of-life sound of laughter.

A series of beeps from the hospital loudspeaker system disturbed the air.

"Your attention, visitors," came the mechanical voice, as it did every night just before eight o'clock. "Visiting hours will be over in five minutes. Attention, visitors. Visiting hours are over in five minutes."

As if a bonfire had just been doused with water, the laughter in Room 713 subsided. No one spoke for a long moment.

"Tell another one, Carlo," Maria said then. "Just one more before you go."

Carlo shook his head. "I don't know any more," he said. "I hate to admit it, but you just heard my best."

"Joey," Mrs. Tirone said, "do you know any?"

Shrugging his shoulders, he replied, "Nope."

Another silent moment ensued. And then a soft voice whispered, "I do."

All heads turned to Donald.

Maria's eyes grew wide. "You do?" she asked.

"Mm-hmm." Donald looked out from behind lowered eyelids.

"So, let's hear it," Carlo said. "Come on. Out with it."

"Yes, Donald, let's hear your joke."

"Yeah, come on."

Donald looked at Maria. She smiled back.

"Okay," he said a little louder. Then he cleared his throat.

"What goes 'ha-ha-ha thump'?"

The Tirones looked at one another. "We give up," Carlo said.

"A man laughing his head off."

Everyone broke into laughter all over again.

"That's the best one yet!" Joey cried.

"I don't get it," Mrs. Tirone said, wiping tears from her eyes.

"Then why are you laughing?" asked Carlo.

"I don't know," his mother replied. "It just sounded so funny. 'Ha-ha-ha thump!' " And the look on her face made everyone laugh even harder.

"Attention, visitors. Visiting hours are now over. Visiting hours are now over."

"Oh, no," Maria cried. "Do you have to go? Stay some more."

"We can't," Mrs. Tirone said. "You know the rules. Besides, I promised Mrs. O'Hearn we'd be home before nine. We'll be back tomorrow."

"I know," Maria said, accepting her mother's kiss. "Tomorrow. But it was fun."

"Yes, it was," her mother whispered in her ear.

As the family was leaving, Carlo asked Donald where he learned his joke.

"Oh, I know lots of them," Donald admitted. "The people who work in the hospital tell them to me all the time. You know, to cheer me up when I'm down. I always try not to smile, but inside I laugh sometimes. And now I know a whole bunch of jokes."

"Well, on our next visit," Mrs. Tirone said, "you'll have to tell us more."

"Okay," Donald agreed eagerly. He was already thinking of which ones he'd tell. After all these years of laughing inside, it felt good to laugh outside as well.

Once the Tirones had left, Donald stayed in Maria's room to play three more games of Bombs Away! Then Mickey, the night nurse, told Donald it was time for him to return to his room.

"Goodnight, Maria," he said at the door.

"Goodnight, Donald. See you tomorrow."

"Yeah. See you tomorrow."

When Donald passed by their station, the nurses couldn't believe their eyes.

He was skipping.

NINE

Dear Joni,

How are you? I am fine. I got your letter in the mail yesterday, and it was neat. I'm sorry Tina went away to visit her aunt and Marlene went on vacation and you're all alone with nobody to play with. I'll try to come home soon.

I've been in the hospital for nine whole days now! I'm standing up straight and I don't have to do any more exercises and real soon they're going to take my stitches out. I hope that doesn't hurt too much.

I have a new roommate named Joanne. She's just a kid (seven), so we don't have a lot in common. She's okay though, I guess. She's having an operation on her ear.

Being in the hospital can get pretty boring. I've read four books, which were pretty good. And I've made a bunch of stuff in the playroom: a painting for Carlo, a painting for Joey (he'll probably just throw it out), and a box for playing cards for Mom and Dad. My *favorite thing is this clay heart I made. I think I'll paint it, but then I'm not sure what to do with it.*

I haven't watched too much TV. Not even "A Better Life."

Most of the time I spend with this kid I met here. His name is Donald.

Well, I hope I'll see you soon.

> *Your friend,*
> *Maria*

"EIGHT . . . nine . . . ten."

Sitting on his bed, Donald finished dealing the cards and put the rest of the pack down, turning the top card face up next to the stack.

"This is a good game," Maria said, across from him. "What's it called again?"

Donald studied his hand carefully. "Gin rummy," he mumbled.

"Oh, yeah. Where'd you learn how to play it anyway?"

"From Mother and Father Schultz. They play it all the time. Now, remember, if you can put all your cards down at one time, you say 'Gin,' and then you get double the score."

"I remember." Maria decided against picking up the card that was face up. Instead, she drew one from the face-down stack. Disappointed in her luck, she said, "Rats." And then, "Donald?"

"Mm-hmm?"

"One time you said your last name was Harris."

"It is."

"So how come you call your mom and dad Mother and Father Schultz?"

Donald sighed and discarded. "Because," he said, "they're not my real mother and father."

"They're not?"

"Uh-uh. They're my foster parents. See, until I was five, I lived with my real mother in this apartment in New York City. Then my real father came to live with us. We didn't get along so well. What I mean is, he hit me a lot. More than my mother ever did. And then, when I was six, the fire happened."

"Where were your mom and dad?"

"Out."

"You were home alone?" Maria asked, surprised. "Didn't you have a babysitter?"

"Nah. They had just gone to the store for food. Anyway, my mom used to leave me alone all the time. Even overnight. Well, sometimes I would stay with Jo and her kids. She was this neighbor lady, and she was real nice." Donald pointed to the watch on the wrist of his braced left arm. "She gave me this for my birthday when I was seven. She was neat. She read me poems when I stayed with her. That's how come I got to like them so much." He paused for a moment, looking up at Maria who was staring at him.

"It's your turn," he said.

"Oh, sorry," Maria answered, picking up a card from the deck.

"So, anyway, when I was six, that's when the fire happened."

Maria remembered what Linda and Bonnie had said about Donald's parents starting the fire in order to kill him.

"Donald?"

"Yeah?"

"How did the fire start? Were you . . . were you playing with matches or something?"

"No, I was asleep. It was an accident. Nobody knows for sure how it started. At least, that's what they told me."

Maria accepted Donald's answer in silence.

"So, anyway, then I was in the hospital for a year."

"A whole year?"

"Uh-huh. While I was there, the judge decided I couldn't live with my mother and father anymore. So I went to live with my first foster family. But that didn't work out so well because they got all up-tight about having a burned kid around. The Carreros, that's the family I was staying with, they had these other kids living there who were handicapped, some of them in wheelchairs and all. But I guess I was too much for them. I didn't look pretty, even if I could walk.

"They tried to get me to wear a wig, but I hated it

and said I wouldn't. I figure you've got to take me the way I am, that's all. No wigs for Donald, like it or not.

"Well, they didn't like it, so I lived with them for only a few months. After the next time I was in the hospital, about three years ago, I came to live with Mother and Father Schultz."

"Are they nice?" Maria asked. "I've never seen them."

"They're okay. They don't come to visit much 'cause they're old and they have trouble getting around. They've come a couple of times, though, and they call me on the phone every day."

"That's good."

"They're not really like parents," Donald continued, "more like grandparents. I guess so, anyway. I don't really know 'cause I never had grandparents. They're kind of strict. But I don't mind. Because at least they don't hit. And they've never tried to make me wear a wig. So, all in all, things are pretty good."

"And you never see your mom? Your real mom, I mean?"

"Nope. I haven't seen her since I was seven."

Maria recalled Donald's poem. She understood now why he called it "A Dream." She looked at him and wondered if he felt as sad as she did just then.

He picked up a card and said, "So now you know the story of my life."

"Yeah," was all she said.

"Gin." Donald broke into a big smile.

"Huh?"

"Gin. I just won the game."

"FASTER! Faster!" Donald cried.

"You want me to have a heart attack?" Maria asked as she pushed Donald in the wheelchair down the long corridor. Her slippers scuffed the polished floor like sandpaper. "Anyway, you're supposed to be saying it while I push."

"Okay. Here I go: 'Which is the wish that wish the wish . . .'"

Maria laughed.

"I'll get it. I just have to concentrate."

Maria turned the wheelchair around at the end of the hall. "Okay," she said, "but this time you'd better get it right. I bet you're just goofing it up so I'll have to keep pushing you."

Donald smiled innocently. "Who, me?" he asked.

"You *are!*" Maria cried. "No fair! Cheater, cheater!"

"Okay, okay. Relax. Let's go."

"All right, but you just better do it."

As Maria pushed him once more down the hall, Donald gleefully shouted, "'Which is the witch that wished the wicked wish?' Perfect!"

Maria brought the wheelchair to a sudden halt. "Perfect," she agreed. "Now it's my turn."

"Okay." Donald and Maria exchanged places, as Donald said, "Remember, I have trouble steering. I can only use one arm."

"Excuses, excuses," Maria retorted. "Okay, I've got my tongue-twister ready. Let's go, captain."

"Aye-aye, sir. Ms. Ma'am. Whatever you are."

Maria loved being wheeled down the corridor, even though Donald's uni-limb steering had brought her perilously close to crashing into the wall several times.

" 'Frisky Frieda feeds on fresh fried fish,' " she called out, as they reached the end of the hall near the nurses' station, and just missed colliding with Gotta Lotta.

"What in heaven's name!" exclaimed the startled nurse, sweeping the tray she was carrying in her hand up and out of the way. "What are you two up to?"

"Nothing," Maria answered, dropping her voice to a whisper.

"Well, it sure don't look like nothin' to me. Donald, you devil, what do you have to say for yourself?"

Donald was silent for the smallest moment. Then he said, "You see, Miz Fielding, we were in the play-room, and Maria said to me, 'Oh, Donald, I have to widdle something awful.' So I grabbed the nearest wheelchair and was trying to rush her back to her room when we bumped into you. I just hope we're not too late."

Gotta Lotta's eyes went wide. She shook her head slowly. "Tsk, tsk, tsk. Maria, I told you to stay away from this one. He is no end of trouble, uh-uh, Lord help us."

Maria bit her tongue to keep from laughing out loud.

"SO there you are," Maria said, letting the playroom door swing shut behind her. "I've been looking everywhere for you."

Donald didn't look up from the sheet of paper on the table in front of him.

"Donald," Maria said, "are you deaf?"

Lorna, who was leaning against the table watching Donald work, raised a finger to her lips. "Shh," she whispered, "he's writing a poem."

"Oh."

Tapping the pencil lightly on the painted wood, Donald seemed deep in thought.

"That's it!" he cried suddenly. "I've got it."

Madly, his pencil raced across the page; with a flourish, the work was complete.

"Ladies and gentlemen," he proclaimed loudly. Then, standing and looking at Lorna and Maria, he said, "Your attention, please. That great poet, Donald Justin Harris, has finished a new masterpiece. It is entitled 'Frogs.'"

" 'Frogs'?" Maria said.

"Sshh! A drumroll, please."

Lorna obliged by playing the tabletop with two magic markers.

"Silence!" Donald commanded.

The drumroll ceased.

Maria and Lorna watched, rapt, as Donald read his new poem aloud.

Being friends with a frog
Means sitting all day on a log.
And if the day gets hot,
You jump in the mud a lot.

You flop around in the oozy slime,
Then hop out to sit in the sun for a time.
Oh, it's fine and it's freeing to be a frog's friend
For flopping and hopping are fun in the end.

Donald bowed deeply. His audience broke into laughter and applause.

"Donald," Lorna said, excitement in her voice, "that is a wonderful poem. It's so clever!"

"Yeah," Maria added, "and it's happy, too."

"I never did one that rhymed before," Donald said. "Was it okay?"

"I love it!" Lorna exclaimed. "Thank you for sharing it with us. May I tape it up on the wall for the other children to see?"

"Sure, why not?" Donald answered, beaming.

And then, though she couldn't be sure, Maria thought she saw something she'd never seen before. She thought she saw Donald blush.

MARIA noticed the boy as they walked down the hall to Donald's room. He must be a new patient, she thought; she was certain she had never seen him before.

"That boy is staring at us," she whispered to Donald.

"Who?" Donald asked.

"That boy," Maria replied, nodding her head in the direction of the boy's bedroom, "the one in the doorway up ahead there."

Donald turned his gaze slightly to the left. The boy, about their age, was gawking openly at them.

"He's not staring at us," Donald explained. "He's staring at *me*. I'll tell him to go to hell."

Maria took her friend's arm and looked into his eyes. "Like you told me, 'take a picture, it'll last longer'? That's no answer. You just end up sounding like you have a chip on your shoulder."

"So what?"

"So who wants to be friends with somebody who's creepy and stuck-up?"

"I don't need to make everybody my friend."

"Yeah, but you don't need to make everybody your enemy, either."

Maria and Donald slowed to a snail's pace as they approached the boy's room.

"So, let's just ignore him," Donald said.

Maria shook her head. "There must be something you can do. Something other than ignoring him or telling him to go to hell."

As if considering the possibility for the first time, Donald thought, maybe there is another way.

As they passed the boy, Donald turned his head

sharply to the left and stuck out his tongue as far as it would go. The boy's jaw snapped shut.

The two picked up their pace and raced the rest of the way to Donald's room. They collapsed, giggling, on the bed.

"Good for you," Maria cried.

Yeah, Donald thought, good for me.

DONALD stopped whistling.

"This is me," he said suddenly. He pointed to the comic book lying open on his lap.

Maria looked up from the Archie comic she was reading, surprised to see the changed expression on Donald's face. "What is?" she asked.

Grimly, Donald extended the comic book in her direction. She took it from him.

"Kids!" the advertisement read. "Now you can become an Ugly Monster! Scare your parents! Terrify your brothers and sisters! Freak out your friends! With Prepco's Magic Monster Make-up Kit, you can make your nightmares come true!" The picture accompanying the ad was of a face so hideously distorted and grotesque that it made Maria suck in her breath. Yet, when she looked closely, there was no denying that to some small degree it did indeed resemble Donald.

"What're you talking about?" she said, without looking up. "This doesn't look like you at all."

"Oh, yes, it does." After a pause, he added, "And if we're going to be friends, don't lie to me, okay?"

Maria didn't say anything then. She just nodded her head slowly and hoped he understood that, though she wanted them to be friends, there were times it was hard not to lie.

"I have a scar, too," was all she could think to say when at last she found her voice.

"I know," Donald answered, "on your chest. It's not the same."

Maria wanted to fight with him then. To say, yes, it is. It *is* the same. We're both freaks. We're both scarred for life.

But then she looked into Donald's eyes and saw the glaze of sadness permanently fired there years before. Vividly, she recalled the mixture of confusion and shock she'd felt when she first beheld the distorted features of Donald's face. You can make your nightmares come true, the ad had read. Every time Donald looks into the mirror, Maria thought, he has to face the bogeyman.

She was angry now. Really angry. But there was no point in fighting with Donald. Because her scar was one thin line. And it was not the same. It was not the same at all.

When Carlo came to see her, she threw her arms around his waist and burst into tears.

"Hey, hey, what's this all about, little sister? What's the matter?"

"Oh, Carlo," she cried, "it isn't fair!"

"What isn't fair?" he inquired gently.

"Nothing's fair. Life isn't fair. God. God isn't fair."

Carlo stroked her hair, letting her cry. After a moment, he said, "What happened, Maria?"

She told him then about the picture in the comic book, about the look on Donald's face when he saw it, about the anger it made her feel.

"Why would God let such a terrible thing happen to Donald, Carlo?"

Carlo sat beside Maria on her bed. His hand held hers as he spoke.

"Maybe God doesn't have control over things like that," he said. "Maybe God is what is good in people, not what goes wrong in their lives."

"Where's God in Donald's life?" Maria asked.

Carlo's reply was a simple one. "Maybe in your being friends with him," he said. "Maybe that's where God is."

He held her hand for a while longer as she thought about what he'd said. She felt very close to him and wished he could stay with her forever.

But he was visiting her on company time; and so, before she was ready, he had to leave.

"Let's talk more like this, you and me," he said, letting go of her hand, "always. Is it a deal?"

"It's a deal," she said. "Cross my heart."

"KNOCK, knock."

"Who's there?"

"Sarah."

"Sarah who?"

"Sarah to say I have to do something yucky to you."

"What?" Maria asked, as Sarah VTI entered her room.

"Well, it's not so yucky, really. I'm here to take your stitches out."

"No," Maria said firmly before she could stop herself.

Sarah threw back her head and laughed. Her long hair, which she wore down today, fell across her shoulders. "No?" she asked, amazed at Maria's defiant response. "What do you mean, no?"

"I don't want you to."

"Why? You keeping them for your dowry or something?"

"I don't even know what that means," Maria answered. "Anyway, don't make jokes."

"Sorry."

"I don't want it to hurt."

Sarah's face became serious. "It won't hurt," she said.

"Sure, sure," Maria retorted. "That's what they all say."

Sarah laughed again. "Boy," she said, "you certainly have turned into a spitfire, haven't you? Okay, listen. I'm going to cut the thread and then pull the stitches out. You'll feel little tugs when I do that, but no pain. I promise. Okay?"

Maria sighed. "Well, it isn't okay. But what choice do I have?"

"None. How clever of you to notice. Okay, off with the pajama top. Hey, where's your roommate?"

Pulling the pajama top up over her head, Maria replied, "In the playroom. Where she always is."

"Can't get enough of that sandbox, huh?"

Maria looked down at her body as Sarah pulled out the stitches. The scar-line ran from her collarbone to the middle of her chest. It was the first time she'd really let herself look at it.

"Will it always be so red?" she asked.

"No," Sarah replied. "A lot of the redness has gone away already. And the swelling's gone down, too. Both will continue to diminish until all that's left is a thin line. Hmm . . ." She leaned forward and examined the scar. "Dr. Ohrne did a beautiful job. You'll have a very neat scar."

"Terrific," Maria said, "let's hear it for Dr. Ohrne. Sarah?"

"Mmm?"

"Will I have normal . . . oh, you know . . ."

Sarah pulled the last stitch. "Okay, all done. That wasn't so bad, was it?"

"No, I guess not."

"You can put your top back on. Now, what were you saying? Will you have normal what?"

Maria watched Sarah toss the stitches into the wastebasket. "Will I have normal breasts?" she asked softly.

"Of course," Sarah answered, taking Maria by the shoulders. "Of course, you will. Your operation had nothing to do with your breasts. Nothing at all."

Later, when she was alone, Maria shut the door of her room and removed her pajama top. Confronting the mirror, which she had carefully avoided for the past two weeks, she studied the long red mark running down her chest. It wasn't *so* bad, she thought after a while. And if Sarah was right, it would look better in time. A long thin line, that's all it would be. Maria felt tremendously relieved.

A knock on the door sent her scurrying from the mirror. The pajama top flew over her head.

"Who is it?" she called out.

"It's me," came the answer. "Donald. Can I come in?"

"Yeah." Maria caught her breath.

The door swung open, and Donald poked his head into the room. "How come you had the door closed?" he asked.

Maria blushed. "No reason."

Donald surveyed the room. "You want to play gin? I brought cards with me, but you have to shuffle."

"Don't I always?" Maria asked, taking the deck of cards and jumping onto the bed. Donald sat down across from her.

"Hey," he said suddenly, "who's fat, wears a red suit and falls down chimneys?"

"I give up."

"Santa Klutz."

Laughing, Maria said, "That's good!"

"I know," said Donald, "I got a million of 'em. Stick with me, kid, and I'll keep you in stitches."

Maria laughed even harder.

"What's so funny now?"

"What you just said," Maria said. "It's too late to keep me in stitches. I just had them taken out!"

"Oh, well," Donald said with a smile. "Stick with me, anyway. Okay?"

"Okay."

Maria dealt the cards, and the game began.

TEN

I T was the morning of Maria's twelfth day in the hospital. She sat in the playroom, quietly painting beside her friend.

"What are you drawing?" she asked.

"Can't you tell?" Donald replied, shifting the piece of paper to the right so Maria could see. On it was a picture of a two-story house. The figure of a man appeared in one of the two windows on the first floor; a woman could be seen in the other. Inside an upstairs window sat a boy looking out at a garden of flowers. Flowers of all sizes and shapes consumed every available inch of the paper not taken up by the house.

"It's really pretty," Maria remarked. "You should color it in, though."

As Donald twisted the sheet of paper back toward himself, he said, "I'm not so good with colors. I can't stay inside the lines."

"That doesn't matter."

"Yes, it does."

"Well, anyway," Maria said, not wanting to argue, "it's pretty. I like all the flowers a lot."

Donald smiled and bent over the table, giving pencil-birth to a daisy.

Maria returned to her clay heart and the white paint with which she was covering it. First, white, she'd decided, then . . . what? She couldn't make up her mind what to paint on it next. Maybe little valentine-shaped hearts in different colors. Maybe stripes. Maybe the words, "Maria's heart." She just didn't know.

A sudden burst of crying interrupted her thoughts. Maria looked over her shoulder to see that it was Joanne making all the noise. Lorna and Dr. Landra were trying to talk to her.

"You have to come with me for just a minute," Dr. Landra was saying. "Then you can come right back to the playroom."

"That's right, sweetheart," Lorna said. "And when you get back, we'll have snack time. Won't that be nice?"

"No," Joanne snapped, stamping her slippered foot on the floor. "I don't want to go. You're going to hurt me."

"No, I'm not," Dr. Landra lied. "I just have to take a little look inside your ear."

With the mention of the word "ear," Joanne screamed even more loudly. "No!" she bellowed, holding onto Lorna for dear life.

Donald said softly to Maria, "How do you get any sleep with a roommate like that?"

"She's not so bad most of the time," Maria answered. "She's scared."

Bob Landra squatted down next to Joanne. "Now, look," he said a little impatiently, "I have to do this. It'll only take a minute. We could do it in here if you like."

Maria stood and started to move toward them.

"Where are you going?" Donald asked.

"I'll be right back."

When she reached Joanne, she looked into the girl's frightened eyes and said, "Lorna and I will be right here, Joanne. Do you want to hold my hand?"

Joanne stopped crying. Returning Maria's deep gaze, she nodded her head slowly. Maria took her hand, accepting the squeeze Joanne gave her as Dr. Landra began to poke about.

"There," he said after a moment, "all done. Now, that didn't hurt, did it?"

"Yes, it did!" Joanne answered, kicking the intern's leg.

"Come, Joanne," Lorna said, standing. "Let's go back to our game of Candyland, shall we?" Joanne nodded. As they turned away, Lorna said to Maria, "Thank you."

"Yeah," Bob Landra said. "That was pretty smart. How'd you think to do that, anyway?"

"Oh, I've been around," Maria replied with a shrug, remembering the words of her former roommate.

Dr. Landra laughed. "Yeah, I guess you have at that," he said. "Well, soon it'll all be behind you. You're going home today."

Maria couldn't believe her ears. "I am?" she asked, astounded.

"Well, sure. Didn't you know?"

"No," Maria answered, grinning broadly. Then the reality of the news hit her full force. "I'm going home!" she cried. "Hurray!"

"Hurray!" echoed Lorna.

"Hurray!" Joanne chimed in.

"Donald, did you hear?" Maria called out. "I'm going home . . ."

Maria turned to see Donald staring at her. His face, blanched to the color of her white clay heart, had the shocked expression of someone who has just been slapped.

Stunned, she watched him rip up the sheet of drawing paper in front of him. Wordlessly, he tore his garden of flowers into shreds.

IT WAS ALL over so suddenly.

Maria looked about her at the room. Stripped of its flowers and stuffed animals, its cards of get-well wishes, its Cara the Cactus and stacks of books and games, it looked like any other hospital room, not the place she'd called home for almost two weeks.

"Now, Maria, you must remember to take it easy," her mother warned as she snapped the suitcase shut.

"No running around for a while, the doctor says. Just go slow, eh?"

"I will," Maria answered.

"What's this?" Mrs. Tirone asked, holding up the strange multi-colored object on the dresser.

Maria crossed quickly to her mother and took the thing from her. "It's nothing," she said, "just something I made in the playroom."

"Well, are you taking it with you? If you are, I'll pack it in the suitcase."

"No, Maria answered. "It's a . . . a present for someone. Mom, when is Carlo coming?"

"Any minute now. And when he gets here, we have to leave right away. 'Cause he's on his lunch hour."

"Then I'll be right back."

Maria darted out the door and down the hall.

"Where are you going?" her mother called after her.

"When Carlo gets here, just tell him I'm in Donald's room," Maria yelled back.

When Maria entered, Donald did not look up from the television show he was watching. For a long moment, neither said a word.

Then, Maria spoke. "Carlo is coming soon," she said. "Then I'm going home." Donald stared straight up at the television. His face seemed to be carved out of rock.

"Well, anyway, I wrote down my address so you can write me," Maria went on. "That is, if you want to. I mean, you don't have to, but if you want to, you should have my address, you know?"

Donald said nothing.

Maria placed the piece of paper with her name and address on the table next to his bed. "I'm putting it here," she said, "on top of this book, okay?" After a pause, she added, "Well, don't you want to give me your address? Even if you don't want to write me, I might want to write you, and how can I if I don't have your addr—"

"Give me a pencil and a piece of paper," Donald said abruptly.

Obligingly, she tore off the bottom half of her sheet of paper and handed it to him with a pencil from the table.

"When are you going home?" she asked as he wrote.

He handed her the paper, which she folded and put in her pocket.

"Soon," he replied. "In a few days."

"Will Mother and Father Schultz come to get you?"

He grunted, and she took it to mean "yes."

Maria sat down on the edge of the chair and looked blankly up at the TV screen. Some kind of cartoon show was on. She was surprised because Donald had once told her he didn't like cartoons. Her gaze drifted to his left arm.

"I'll bet you'll be glad to get that brace off, huh?"

"Yep."

"How much longer do you have to wear it?"

"I told you, a couple of months. The one on my neck, too."

"Wow," Maria said. Then she couldn't think of another thing to say. After a moment, she became aware of the object on her lap. It was her clay heart, now brightly painted with flowers.

"I have a present for you," she announced. Donald's head turned slightly, then stopped. She stood, extending her gift close enough to him that he could see, yet far enough away that he could not take it without reaching.

He shifted his eyes until the thing came into view. Then he reached for it and put it down on his chest.

"It's what you were painting," he said.

"Yes."

"What is it, anyway?"

"It's my heart," she replied. "I know it's not pretty, but it's what a real heart looks like. Sort of. And it has a patch inside just like my heart does. I put the flowers on . . . well, just 'cause I wanted to."

Donald examined it for a long time. "Thanks," he said at last, "it's nice. But I don't have a present for you."

"Oh, that's okay," she replied too quickly. "It doesn't matter."

In the long silence that followed, Maria wished that Donald did have a present for her. She wanted something to remember him by. Something to pick up and look at, like her clay heart. And then she started thinking about things she wished she could say. Like how glad she was they'd become friends. Like how much she'd miss him. But somehow no words were coming, and everything in her head began to feel like a scrambled mess. She watched as a cartoon mouse slammed a frying pan over the head of a cartoon cat. She wished she could smash the silence as easily.

"Hey, hey, hey," the big brother voice called from the door. "Got to get moving."

Maria turned to see Carlo entering the room.

"What's on TV?" he asked.

Donald just shrugged his shoulders.

"Hey, Donald, did you hear this one? What did the three-hundred pound mouse say?"

"Here, kitty-kitty," Donald answered without cracking a smile. "I heard it." He didn't even look in Carlo's direction.

Carlo let out a sound that was somewhere between a sigh and a whistle. "I guess you did," he said.

He touched Maria lightly on the shoulder. "I'm sorry to have to rush you, kiddo, but I've got to move."

"I know," Maria said softly.

Carlo looked from his sister to Donald and back again. "I'll go get your stuff. Meet you at the elevator, okay?"

"Okay."

He moved to the door and turned back. "Hey, Donald," he called out.

This time, Donald looked up at him. "Yes?"

"Keep learnin' those jokes. I want to hear some new ones the next time I see you."

"The next time, huh?" Donald snorted. "Sure."

"That's a promise now," Carlo said.

Donald smiled slightly. "Okay."

As soon as Carlo disappeared, Donald's smile vanished, too. He continued to stare at the television set.

"Well, goodbye," Maria said. "I hope you get to go home real soon."

Donald said nothing. For a fleeting second, he glanced at Maria, then back at the cartoon images on the screen.

"Goodbye," he said in no particular tone of voice at all.

Confused, Maria left the darkened room and walked down the long corridor to where she saw her mother and brother waiting in the distance. As she approached them, she could hear the sound of clicking behind her. First slow. Then faster and faster. She knew that Donald was pressing the remote control button, wildly flipping the channels on the television set.

In his own way, he was smashing the silence.

ELEVEN

WALKING down Oak Avenue with her friends on a bright Saturday morning, Maria could hardly believe she'd ever been in the hospital at all. It seemed such a long time ago, though it had been only a week. Joni and Tina had taken to calling her "Santa Maria" after she'd shown them her scar.

"Ai, Maria," Tina had squealed squeamishly as she beheld the line down Maria's chest, "you're so brave."

"A saint," Joni had added, "that's what you are."

"It's the truth," Tina concurred. "Santa Maria."

And when she'd told them all about her surgery and the tubes running in and out of her, they'd cried, "Oh, gross," and "poor Maria," and she'd enjoyed every minute of it.

They couldn't believe she'd missed two whole weeks of "A Better Life." "What did you *do* in the hospital all that time?" Tina'd asked. Maria had told them then about the playroom and Linda and Bonnie and Lorna and . . . her special friend.

"Did you get a letter from Donald yet?" Tina asked as they turned the corner into the park.

"No," Maria said. She'd written him the first day she was home and was still waiting to hear from him. Maybe he wasn't her friend anymore. She wasn't sure what to think.

"What? No letter from your boyfriend? You'd better get yourself a new one."

Maria stopped and faced her friends. "I told you, he's not my boyfriend. He's just a friend."

"Who happens to be a boy," Tina giggled.

"What was he in the hospital for, anyway?" Joni asked. "You never told us."

"He was burned," she said.

"Oooo," Tina said somewhere in the back of her throat. "Where? On his arm? I knew somebody who was burned on his arm once."

"All over," Maria answered.

Joni asked, "What do you mean 'all over'?"

"All over. His arms, his chest, his head, his face. Everywhere practically."

"His face!" Tina shrieked. "Oh, gross. What did he look like? I know, I'll bet he looked like this." She pulled down the corners of her eyes and mouth while pushing up her nose.

"Stop it!" Maria cried. "That isn't fair. He can't help how he looks. He was burned in a fire!"

"But how could you be friends with someone like that? Just the thought of it gives me the creeps."

"You don't know anything about 'someone like that,' Tina," Maria said angrily. "Just because he doesn't look so great doesn't mean he can't be somebody you can like. I was afraid you guys wouldn't like me because of the scar on my chest. But you still like me, don't you?"

"Yeah," Tina admitted. "But that isn't the same."

"I know it isn't the same. But what is the same is that Donald is still a person, just like I'm a person."

"Maria's right," Joni said.

"He's more than just a person, he's my friend. And I don't want you making fun of him."

"Okay, okay," Tina said, backing away. "Boy, calm down, will you?"

Joni put her arm around Maria's shoulders.

"I didn't mean to yell," Maria said. "But it makes me mad."

"I'm sorry I made fun," Tina said. She looked into Maria's eyes. "Still friends?"

After a moment, Maria nodded her head. "Still friends," she said.

"Maria!" Marlene called out from the swings. The three girls ran to her. "Maria! You're back. Oh, Maria!"

"Santa Maria, if you please," Tina insisted as she bumped into Joni's backside. The three girls walked to the nearest bench and sat down. Marlene stood, blowing bubbles with her gum as punctuation.

"Maria, you look so *good!*" (bubble), she exclaimed. "You see?" she went on, turning to Joni and Tina, "I told you she'd be okay. No sweat."

"Oh yeah, no sweat, huh?" Joni said. "First you told her she was going to get somebody else's heart—"

"—which she didn't," Tina interjected.

"—and then once she was in the hospital, you practically had her dead and buried."

"Yeah," Tina said turning to Maria, "Marlene had this long discussion one day—"

"Stop it!" (bubble), Marlene said.

Not allowing the distraction, Tina went on, "—this discussion about what she was going to wear to your funeral."

"Oh, no," Maria said, appalled and fascinated at the same time.

" 'Black is so hot in the summer,' " Tina persevered, her imitation of Marlene right on target, " 'and besides, it just isn't my color. Do you think Maria would hate me if I wore orange?' "

"Oh, Marlene," Maria said, extending her arm and dramatically dropping her hand at the wrist, "I'd be thrilled if you wore orange at my funeral. It's so *you,* darling. So daring!"

Joni picked up on Maria's game. "Though perhaps you should wear a touch of black. Just to be proper, don't you know. Orange and black would be so you. So . . . so Halloween!"

All three girls laughed openly at Marlene, whose only response was to storm off and throw an outraged look over her shoulder. "Well," she called out, "I'll have to tell Maria another time what happened to *me* while she was away!"

"Oh, poor Maria," Tina said, giggling, as they watched Marlene's retreat, "you're not going to hear the saga of Marlene and her never-ending period."

"I'll live," Maria replied lightly.

"How can you say such a thing?" Joni asked. "Now Marlene won't be able to wear her orange and black outfit until Halloween."

Joni and Tina began to giggle. But Maria didn't. Suddenly, without conjuring the thought, she saw Donald's face. She heard his voice saying, "That's me," as he handed her the comic book with the ad for monster make-up. "That's me," reverberated in her head as she wondered where Donald was now, if he was still in the hospital or if he'd gone home. Where was he, and was he still her friend?

"Mar-ee-a," Tina called, waving her hand before Maria's vacant eyes, "Santa Mar-ee-a."

"What are you thinking about?" Joni asked. "You look like you're out in space."

"Nothing," Maria replied softly.

"Well, then, what's the matter?" Tina inquired. "You're so down in the dumps all of a sudden. Hey, I've been practicing that tongue-twister you taught me. Want to hear?"

Church bells tolled in the distance.

"Lunchtime," Tina said. "I gotta go. I promised my

mom I'd make lunch for everybody so she could go shopping. You guys want to come to my house?"

"Okay," said Joni.

Maria thought for a moment. She really wanted to go home to see if a letter had come in the mail. "Maybe I'll come over later," she said. "I've gotta go home first."

"Okay," said Tina. "You'll have to wait to hear that tongue-twister then. See you later."

"Bye."

"Bye, Maria."

Walking up Laburnam Avenue alone, Maria was so lost in thought that at first she didn't notice the car moving slowly behind her. When it honked, she jumped.

Old yellow Chevy convertible, she thought, as she took in the car surreptitiously. The guy driving wore sunglasses, but she didn't really look too closely. Better not to. Better just to keep moving. Never talk to strange men in cars, her mother had often warned her. And with the things you read about in the newspapers these days, she knew it to be good advice.

"Honk!"

Maria didn't look back. She kept her eyes fixed straight in front of her. She could feel her heart pounding. What does this guy want, anyway? Great, she thought, I live through open-heart surgery only to be bumped off by some crazy nut in a convertible. And right on my own block!

The car pulled alongside of her, and she noticed then that there was writing on the side.

" 'Easy Goin' '," the lettering read.

"Honk!"

Maria turned her head sharply, and no longer listening to her mother or her own inner voice, she stared the driver full in the face.

"Carlo!"

"Well, it's about time," Carlo said. "I was beginning to think you didn't know me anymore."

"I didn't recognize you with those sunglasses on, and . . . wait a minute!" She and the car came to a halt. "This is it, isn't it?" she cried excitedly. "You got your car."

"I got *our* car," Carlo corrected. "Hop in. I'll take you for a ride."

Maria opened the door and jumped in.

"Oh, Carlo. A convertible! I just love it. It's so cool. Wait until Joni and Tina see this. They'll just die!"

"Oh, no!" Carlo said. "Not those two! I'm not ready for them yet, jabbering away in the back seat. We'll take them for a ride another time. Where were you going, anyway?"

"Home."

"Well, that'll be a short ride. But if that's where you want to go . . ."

"No, no, I don't have to. I was just going to see if . . ." Maria stopped herself when she saw the long white envelope lying on the seat between her and Carlo. "Maria Tirone" the envelope read.

"Oh, I almost forgot," Carlo said then, pushing the envelope toward her. "I just picked up the mail, and this letter came for you."

Maria studied the front of the envelope. She was sure she recognized the handwriting. And the postmark did say "Brewster."

She turned it over. "D.J. Harris, c/o Schultz." Hurriedly, she tore the envelope open, removing the two sheets of lined paper from inside.

Carlo passed the Tirone residence, continuing down Laburnam Avenue as Maria read the letter.

Dear Maria,

How are you? I am feeling pretty good. I came home on Tuesday. Mother and Father Schultz came to get me. Everything has been okay here, except I still have to wear these braces, like I told you. I hate them and can't wait until they come off.

Things were okay in the hospital after you left. I had a fight with Gotta Lotta one day about eating that junky food, but what else is new? Judy showed me some exercises to do when I get the braces off. Oh, and Lorna said to say hi when I wrote to you.

I didn't have a present for you when you left because I didn't feel like anything I made would be very good. I have what you gave me on my desk. It makes a good paperweight. Anyway, I wrote this poem and I hope

you like it, even if it isn't something you can do any-
thing with. It's just me and my words.

Thanks for writing. Will you write me again?

Your friend,
Donald

P.S. You are the best friend I ever had.

Maria looked up for a moment and noticed they'd turned down Robinson Street. It was an ordinary block, just like all the others in her neighborhood, but to her it seemed just then as if it had been cleaned to a shine and was drying in the midday sun.

Then she pulled the second sheet of paper out from behind the first and read what was written there.

"The Night Maria Became My Friend," the poem was called.

The sky was endless black that night
Dreamy, dreamless black
Without a ray of light
*   Without a star*
And I could see . . . nothing.
Then . . . I did not know how or why . . .
Stars began to leak through the night sky.
First here, then there
Pinpricking the heavens
*   Letting the sleeping sun seep through.*
And the blackness was flooded with light,
Night became brighter than the brightest day.

I held up my hands
Waved them about in the star-struck way
Of a person who is blinded by the joy of seeing.
And for the first time in that long, dark night . . .
I could see.

Maria thought for a long time about the poem. At first, she wasn't sure she understood it. What did shining stars have to do with her being Donald's friend? Then she remembered what Carlo had said to her about God in Donald's life maybe being her friendship with him. And it all made sense then in a funny sort of way.

"Is it a good letter?" Carlo asked, jolting her from her reverie.

"Mmm," she murmured, thinking she might share it with him sometime. For now, it belonged to her alone.

"You're glad to hear from Donald, eh?"

"Uh-huh. Carlo?"

"Yeah?"

"You know when we left the hospital, and I was sad, like?"

"Yes."

"Well, it was because of Donald. He acted so weird when I said goodbye. I thought he didn't like me anymore."

"He was probably angry to be losing you. My guess is that Donald doesn't have a lot of friends. You were someone special . . ."

"His best friend, he says."

"Uh-huh. And maybe he never even had a best friend before in his whole life. He must have felt real bad to get a best friend like you and then lose you."

Maria recalled what Lorna had said to her about making friends in the hospital and then having to lose them.

"He's my friend, too," she said. "I didn't want to lose him either."

"Did you tell him that?"

"I wanted to, but . . . I don't know. I got all mixed-up. I thought he was mad at me. I didn't understand what was going on."

"So why don't you write him and tell him how you felt?"

"Yeah, I could do that," Maria said, considering the suggestion. Then an even better idea occurred to her. It was a wonderful idea.

"Carlo," she said excitedly.

"Yeah?"

"Is this really our car? Yours and mine?"

"Sure."

"And it can take us anywhere we want to go?"

"It's our escape-mobile," Carlo answered, laughing. "It might not get us to the moon, but other than that . . ."

"Can it get us to Brewster?"

Carlo pulled up to a traffic light and stopped. "Well, sure, I guess. That's about an hour from here, I think. Maybe a little more."

"Good. Then, that's where I want to go."

"Now?" Carlo looked into his sister's eyes. He saw all that he needed to see to make up his mind. "Why not?" he said, as the light turned green and he drove through.

"Really? Do you know how to get there?"

"I can find out."

"Oh, neat! Just wait until Donald sees us. He'll be so surprised!" Maria collapsed against the seat, affectionately patting the black leather upholstery next to her. "This is just about the best car in the whole wide world," she said.

Carlo smiled. "You're not so bad yourself," he told her.

After stopping to ask directions at a gas station, they set out on their way. Maria stretched her legs, lightly tapping her feet in rhythm to the music, which played softly on the radio. The wind tossed her hair about her forehead and ears. She squinted into the sun and felt her cheeks grow warm.

One journey ended. Another begun.